The Other Country

The Other Country

Legends and Fairy Tales of Scotland

Retold by
Marion Lochhead

HAMISH HAMILTON
London

Copyright © 1978 Marion Lochhead

First published in Great Britain 1978 by
Hamish Hamilton Children's Books Ltd
90 Great Russell Street, London WC1B 3PT

ISBN 0 241 89773 4

Printed in Great Britain by
Cox & Wyman Ltd, London, Fakenham and Reading

Chapter heading design by
SALLY HOLMES

Contents

Introduction

Every country has its history and geography. There is also another, inner or secret country known to its people long before history was written or maps were drawn: the Other Country of legends and fairy tales. This too has its history: stories of the fairies, the elves, The Good People, The Other People (they have many names). There is even some geography of this kingdom. Those Other People are said to live within the hills, or, some of them, the sea-folk, in the sea or a loch.

For centuries in Scotland this history has been told in stories by the fire, in Highland and in Lowland and Border country cottages; told by people who had no book-learning, could, many of them, neither read nor write, but who had strong memories which held all they had been told about that Other Country and its people. There were wandering story-tellers too, who brought tales from many regions.

Later on, within the past three hundred years, there have been men with book-learning who heard and cherished these stories, collected and published them. Something is told about these good scholars at the end of this book.

The Other Country, like the country we know, had its laws. Most of the tales have a moral. Certain virtues are very important, such as obedience. The hero or heroine may be told: "You must not" do this or that; and disobedience, even slight, brings a penalty. For the poor girl in *The Black Bull of Norroway* a very tiny bit of disobedience, really no more than forgetfulness, brought seven long years of searching for her lost love.

Courtesy is very important. The son who begs his mother's blessing in *The Red Etin* is lucky; his brothers who go off without it fall into misfortune.

There is courtesy also between humans and birds and beasts. The latter are often very kind and helpful: like the fox in the story of *Prince Ian Direach*, the eagle in *The Kingdom of the Green Mountains*, the crow in

The Hoodie Crow, where the youngest sister breaks the spell that held him in bird form.

It is not always good to ask too many questions or to go too far or know too much. Nor is it wise to invite any of those Other People into the house. They have their secrets. The story of Inary, *The Good House-wife*, shows how foolish it can be to ask for fairy help.

These stories are very old and have been told and published many times, but a good tale is worth retelling in new words. May they bring you pleasure now.

Some Scottish words which appear in the tales

Ahint: behind

Ain: own

Aince: once

Bairn: child

Bannock: oatmeal cake or biscuit

Ben: in; into the inner room of the house; *but* and *ben* are the kitchen and the room behind it

Bide: stay, wait

Birk: birch tree

Brae: low hill

Brochan: broth, soup

Brose: a kind of pudding made with oatmeal, or more often peasemeal, and water

Canny, cannily: cautious, cautiously

Cauld: cold

Ding: strike

Fauld: sheep- or cow-fold

Greet: cry or sob

Joup: skirt or gown; like French *jupe*

Haly: holy

Kail: soup or broth made of cabbage or other vegetables

Ken: know

Kitchen: to add something savoury to plain bread

Kittle: litter, produce its young

Leal: loyal or faithful

Mirk: dark. *Mirk night:* the darkest part of the night

Or: ere, before

Sark: shirt

Siccan: such

Snell: sharp or keen, describing cold air or wind

Snood: a ribbon round the head

Snouk: smell

Stane: stone

Tide: happen

Warlock: wizard

Rashiecoat

There was once a princess who was lovely, good and gay, and a lass of spirit, besides. She was dutiful, but would not be ordered about. So, when her father bade her marry a man she disliked, she said politely but very firmly:

"Thank you, father, but I'd rather not have him."

"Don't talk like that to your father. It does not matter whether or not you like him. You will marry him," the king told her angrily. The princess had no mother; the queen had died two or three years before.

Very sensibly the girl did not argue. She went to the hen-wife and asked her advice, for the hen-wife was a wise woman.

"Say you will marry this man if he will give you a gown of beaten gold," suggested the hen-wife, and the princess made this demand.

The would-be bridegroom, who was a very rich prince, got her a gown of the finest beaten gold, smooth and fine as silk. In it the girl, with her golden-brown hair and rose-leaf complexion, looked lovelier than ever.

"Why can't you marry him?" everyone said. "Not many bride-grooms could give you a gown like that. He is rich and powerful; he will give you rare jewels besides."

The princess went back to the hen-wife, who told her:

"Say you will marry him if he will give you a gown woven from the feathers of every bird of the air."

The princess asked for that and she was given it. The would-be bridegroom sent a man to spread a great sheet on the ground; he whistled a tune which compelled every bird of the air to come flying and to swoop down, leaving a feather on the sheet. They were gathered up and woven together by a most skilful woman into an incredibly lovely web. In it were the shining blue-black feather of the raven, the gold and green of the finch, blue from the kingfisher, brown and speckled from the sparrow and the thrush, red from the robin's breast, dove-grey and pink—every colour you can think of.

"Who else could have given you such a wonderful gown? You must marry him now," everyone told the princess, who said nothing at all but went again to the hen-wife.

"Ask him for a gown woven from the green rushes, and a pair of slippers."

The princess asked the man for the new gown and the slippers, and they were given her. It sounds a less gorgeous gown than the one of beaten gold or of the feathers from every bird of the air, but when she wore it she looked even lovelier than in those splendid garments. The willow-green set off her colouring of golden-brown and rose and white; she looked like a fairy princess. "Rashiecoat" they all called her when she appeared (*rashie* means a rush, and *coat* here means a gown) and told her that she must now marry the man. "Marry him tomorrow," added the king, her father, sternly.

Sadly the princess went to the hen-wife, but this time she had no help.

"There's no more I can tell you, so you'd better make up your mind to have him."

That the princess would not or could not do. She packed her three gowns and the slippers in a bag, put on a rough dress and cloak and shoes, and ran away, travelling until she came to the house of another king, far enough from her father's to be safe. Here she asked to be given work and was taken into the kitchen to help the cook. Rashiecoat, as she was now called, had to work hard, clearing and laying the fire on the hearth, fetching wood and water, washing pots and dishes, doing everything the cook ordered her to do. She was given the left-over food to eat, she had to sleep in a tiny room no better than a cupboard, but she took it all so cheerfully, did every task so willingly and well that the cook began to like her, and treated her well, gave her plenty to eat and let her help with the cooking, even with that for the king's own table. And one Sunday morning the cook said:

"They are all away to the kirk, and I want to go too. I'll leave you to look after the dinner."

The king and queen with their son the prince had driven away in their coach, the ladies and courtiers followed, the servants, including the cook, all went too, some riding, some walking; only Rashiecoat was left behind to watch the broth-pot, turn the roast on the spit, keep an eye on the apple-pie in the oven and generally look after the house.

Almost at once there came into the kitchen a little old woman who looked very kindly at Rashiecoat.

"Good day to you, my dear."

"And good day to yourself, ma'am," answered Rashiecoat, with a curtsy.

"And why are you not at the kirk with the rest of them?"

"I am left to mind the dinner."

"Well, I'll do that for you, my dear. Go now and wash from head to foot, brush your bonny hair and put on your golden gown."

Rashiecoat willingly did as she was told, and very lovely she looked.

"Now," said the little old woman, "you will find a coach waiting to take you to the kirk. Leave just after the blessing, before anyone else has time to move, and the coach will bring you back. And my blessing go with you. I am your godmother, my dear. I was at your christening, your dear mother was my friend."

Rashiecoat curtsied again and thanked the kind old woman. The coach was there, the coachman on his seat. He drove her so swiftly that she was in the kirk before the first prayer was said. People looked at her, wondering who this lovely lady in her golden gown could be. Rashiecoat sat at the back of the kirk, and at the end of the service, as soon as the blessing had been given, she slipped out. The coach awaited her, the coachman drove off swiftly, she had time to change into her old dress again and was busy in the kitchen when the cook and the other servants came in, all talking about this strange beautiful lady, a princess she must be, who had come to the kirk and gone again so quickly. They noticed nothing strange about Rashiecoat. The godmother had, of course, disappeared, but she had looked after the dinner. The broth-pot was simmering, the roast was perfectly done, the apple-pie was crisp.

"That's a good lass," said the cook, and she saw to it that her kitchen-maid had a good dinner herself.

Next Sunday it all happened again. Rashiecoat was left to see to the dinner; her godmother came in, and bade her put on her gown of feathers from every bird of the air. In this, with its shades and ripples of every colour, she looked even lovelier than before and the kind godmother was very pleased.

The coach was waiting; she was driven to the kirk in time, she left as soon as the blessing was given and was back in the kitchen before anyone else had returned. But this time the prince had noticed her particularly; in fact he had sat looking at her, hoping that she might be presented to the queen; but before the kirk skailed or emptied, she had gone and none had seen her go or could tell anything about her.

On the third Sunday it happened as before.

"Put on your gown of rashes," the godmother told her. In this she looked still more beautiful than in the golden gown or in the gown of feathers of every colour. The prince saw her come in, he did not take his eyes from her. The queen had to touch him to make him stand and kneel at the proper moments. Rashiecoat saw this, and she slipped out just before the end of the service, got into the coach and was driven off; indeed she moved so quickly that one of her slippers fell off and the prince picked it up.

Now the king and queen had for some time been urging their son to marry. They had introduced more than one suitable bride, but the prince would have none of them. He told them that day that he would marry the girl who could wear the slipper.

Whatever the king and queen thought they said nothing but agreed, and a messenger was sent out with a proclamation from the king that all unmarried girls might come to the palace and try on the slipper.

A great many came, but none could fit the slipper on her foot. At the princess's home the hen-wife heard about it, and she said to her daughter (an ugly wench but neither she nor her mother thought so):

"Why would you not go and try on the slipper?"

"I will; and I'll make it fit," declared the daughter, and off she went.

Her foot was too big but she hacked at the heel and the big toe until she could cram it into the slipper. The prince was horrified, but he must keep his promise. He took the girl up behind him on his horse and rode off to the kirk to be married, leaving poor Rashiecoat busy in the kitchen, helping the cook to prepare a wedding-feast for which no one had any appetite.

The way to church led through a wood. The prince rode silent and gloomy, the girl was full of pride. A bird was singing on a tree. As he rode, the prince could hear the song clearly and every word in it:

> "Nippit foot and clippit foot
> Ahint the prince rides;
> But bonny foot and slender foot
> Ahint the cauldron bides."

The prince stopped, listened, turned his horse and rode quickly back to the palace, paying no heed to the wench bawling and screeching behind him.

He dismounted, and rushed in—not into the great hall but into the kitchen, and there, by the cauldron on the hearth stirring the broth, he saw Rashiecoat, and knew her at once, in spite of her old gown, for the lovely lady he had seen and loved in the church. Taking her by the hand, he kissed her, and led her to the king and queen who, realizing that there must be a fairy godmother somewhere, and recognizing a princess even in a shabby and dusty old gown, welcomed his bride, and gave glad consent to the marriage.

After that, everything happened very quickly. The godmother appeared, Rashiecoat was dressed in her gown of green rushes and driven off to the kirk. Everyone in the palace followed. The cook said:

"I aye thocht she was a princess."

which was not perhaps true, but she had been kind, and Rashiecoat did not forget that. There was a splendid wedding-feast (perhaps the godmother lent a hand) and everyone was radiant—except the hen-wife and her daughter. What happened to them? They went off to their own home unnoticed. They do not matter.

After the feast there was a ball. They all danced until their shoes were worn out, all except Rashiecoat's. She and the prince were happy all their life, and that is the end of the story.

2

The Hoodie Crow

There were three sisters once, and they were washing clothes one day by the river. A black hoodie crow flew over, and dropped down beside them.

"Will you marry me?" he asked the eldest girl.

"Marry you—an ugly creature like you? Indeed I will not," she answered rudely.

Next day they were at their work again, and the hoodie crow came back.

"Will *you* marry me?" he asked the second girl.

"You—the ugliest creature I've ever seen! Certainly not!" said she.

On the third day he came again and asked the third sister who was also the prettiest and much the nicest:

"Will *you* marry me?"

"I will," she said, "you pretty creature."

This pleased the hoodie very much, and next day they were married; then he said to her:

"I am under a spell and maybe one day it will be broken. But for now—I can be a man by day, a crow by night, or a crow by day and a man by night. It is for you to say."

"I'd have you a man by day and a hoodie by night," said his bride, and at once he turned into a fine, tall, handsome man.

He took her off to his own house, a fine one, and he was a good, kind husband. They were happy together, and happier still when a son was born to them. But the happiness was brief; for, the night after the baby's birth, fine music was heard, playing all round the house; music too lovely for mortals to make or mortals to hear, and they all fell asleep. When they awoke, the baby was gone, and there was sore grief.

Time went on and another child was born to them, as bonny as the first. Their joy returned, but not for long. Again in the night, spell-binding music was heard, and again they all slept under the spell and awoke to find the child gone; and again there was sorrow. Before the year was out they had a third son. A watch was set in and around the house, but in vain. The magic music bound them all in sleep, and this baby too, like his brothers, was stolen away.

"Let us be leaving this house," said the hoodie-husband. "I must take you to another I have, and maybe the enchantment will not follow us. Be sure that you take with you everything I have ever given you."

They set out in a coach and on the way the husband said to his wife:

"Are you sure you have not forgotten anything?"

"I have forgotten my comb," she said; and at once the coach turned into a withered branch and her husband took his hoodie shape and flew away, so there was the poor lady alone.

But she was a brave lady, and she went on by herself, walking as fast as she could. She could see her hoodie-husband flying ahead, but never came up with him. When she saw him on a hill-top she climbed the hill, but when she came to the top, there he was down in the valley beyond. All day she trudged, and at nightfall came to a little house with light from fire and candle glowing in it. As she stood at the door she saw within a wee boy to whom her heart yearned. There was a woman there who welcomed her kindly, gave her food, water to wash in, and a bed for the night.

In the morning she rose and went on her way. The hoodie was to be seen, always flying ahead of her, and she followed bravely until night-fall when again she came to a little house, warm and bright; and she saw there a younger child, playing on the floor, over whom she yearned. There was a kind woman there too, who gave her food and shelter, and next morning she went on her way.

This third day passed like the others, she following the hoodie and he always flying ahead of her. This third night she came to a house of welcome and there saw a baby in a cradle by the hearth, whom she longed to hold and nurse. The woman of the house welcomed her with good news.

"Your man has been here, and he will come again tonight. Do not sleep, but stay awake, and when he comes, seize him and hold him."

The poor lady tried to keep awake but she had travelled many miles and was utterly tired. She fell asleep; her hoodie-husband came to her and slipped a ring on her finger. This woke her, she saw him and tried to catch him. But she was too late; he flew off, under enchantment, leaving a wing-feather in her hand.

Now she was in grief and despair, not knowing what to do. The kind woman of the house comforted her:

"He is not lost to you, though he is far away, and you will have a long and dangerous way to go. He has flown over a hill where the ground is poisonous, and you cannot climb it except with iron shoes on your feet. First you must go to the smith and learn to make them."

This the brave girl did; and so eager and so clever was she that she learned quickly, and made herself a pair of iron shoes. Shod with them she walked safely and swiftly up the hill of poison, and down into the town in the valley beyond; and there the first news she heard was of a knight once enchanted, now returned to his true shape. This must be her husband, but he had not returned to his true mind: for he was to be married to a lady there, the daughter of a nobleman, and he seemed to have forgotten his own true wife.

This poor, brave lady went to the nobleman's house. There were great doings in the town before the wedding; there were to be sports and races, and the cook was eager to leave his work and go.

"Can you cook?" he asked the wandering lady.

"I can," said she.

"Then will you cook the dinner and let me go to the sports?"

"I'll do that gladly." She saw a way to win back her husband.

She cooked the dinner and served it. When she served the broth she dropped the ring and the feather into the bridegroom's plate. With the first spoonful he took up the ring and some of his memory came back; with the second he took up the feather, and all his memory came back. He knew that only one person, his own true wife, could have put the ring and the feather there.

"Who made this broth?" he asked.

The cook was home from the games now and was summoned.

"But *I* did not make the broth," he said. "It was this lass here."

The brave girl came forward; her husband knew her and took her in his arms.

"This is my own true wife," he said, "whom I have lost for a while by enchantment. But now we are together, and we must go away."

And with little more ado he went off with her, and what the noble-man and his daughter thought has not been told, and need not concern us.

The lady and her husband climbed the hill, he carrying her on his back and wearing the iron shoes. In this way neither of them ever set naked foot on the poisoned ground. They came safely over, and back to the house where the kind woman had given her help and counsel. And there was the baby in the cradle and he was their own son; and the woman was the husband's own sister, who had done all she could to help them. That night they stayed with her in happiness, and next day went on to the second house, where the woman was the husband's second sister, taking care of the second wee son; the third night, as you have guessed, they came to the first house where the boy was running about outside the door; their own first-born.

Now they were all together again, and they came home to their own house in great joy, to live happily to the end of their days.

The Kingdom of the Green Mountains

There were three soldiers once, who, their service being ended, went wandering through the wide world in search of their fortune. After a time they decided to part ways, each to follow his own, hoping to meet in the end. The first was a sergeant, the second a corporal, the third a private.

After walking for a day or two the sergeant came to a fine, big house, a palace indeed, and being tired and hungry thought he would beg food and shelter for the night. He was not turned away; a beautiful lady greeted him.

"You'll have many a good story to tell," said she. "So come you in and I'll have supper brought to you."

This was good hearing, and the sergeant followed her into a grand room where a table was set, lit by candles. Food was brought at once, rich food and good wine; the sergeant's hunger grew.

"Choose what you like," said the lady. "But forgive me if I put out the candles. It is our custom here."

"Sure if that is your custom I have nothing against it," he said. "And I am grateful for the good supper you are putting before me."

He began to eat. The lady put out the candles, but before he had swallowed more than a mouthful, she struck her foot on the floor—which brought two servants in.

"Take this rascal and lock him up," she commanded. "Feed him on bread and water and nothing else."

They obeyed her and the poor man was shut up in darkness.

Next night the corporal arrived at the same fine house, and he too begged food and shelter. He too was welcomed by the lady, and brought into the room where the table was set and lit by candles.

"You will be hungry," said the lady. "I shall have supper brought to you."

A good supper was brought and the lady told him to choose what he liked best.

"Then I must put out the candles," she said, "for it is our custom here."

"If it is your custom it is not for me to say anything against it," replied the corporal politely. He began to eat, but had swallowed no more than a mouthful when the lady summoned her servants and had him too shut up in a dungeon with only bread and water for food and drink.

On the third night came the private; he had wandered farther than the others and was very weary and hungry. He was kindly welcomed. A fine supper was served; the lady had the same story about putting out the candles; as soon as she did so the private, without waiting to eat a morsel, got up, caught her round the waist and kissed her.

"It is a good supper," he said, "but you are sweeter than any food and more rare than any wine."

The lady struck the floor with her foot; her servants came but she did not order them to seize and take away the private. Instead, she told them:

"Bring more candles, and wait upon us at supper."

She and the soldier sat down together and feasted. He had many a good tale to tell her which she liked very well.

"Have you had any schooling?" she asked.

"I have that," he said.

"Can you write a good hand?"

For answer he wrote his name in a good, clear hand.

"Will you marry me?" she asked, going straight to the point.

"I will, with pleasure," said he with equal directness.

"You must know that I am a princess, the only daughter of the King of the Green Mountains. I have gold and jewels. I could marry a prince or a king, but I have no wish to do so. I would rather marry a lad like yourself, of common birth but good sense and manners, education and looks."

"Well, that pleases me more than anything I've heard," said the soldier gallantly.

The princess then showed him to a fine bedroom where he slept very well. In the morning they met at breakfast and made plans for their wedding.

"Take this purse of gold," said the lady. "Go to the tailor in the town yonder and bid him make you a fine suit of clothes. Wait till it is ready, then come back to me."

The soldier obeyed very willingly. He found the tailor who was skilled in his craft and very soon made him a suit of the finest cloth which fitted him perfectly. He paid the tailor and prepared to set off. The princess was to meet him, in her coach, at one part of the road.

Now the tailor had a crafty old mother, little better than a witch.

"Go with the soldier," she told her son. "Talk to him and keep him entertained. When he says he is tired and thirsty, and sits down to rest, as he will, give him this apple."

The tailor did as he was told. He walked some way with the soldier and amused him with his talk. As they came to the meeting-place the soldier said:

"Och, but I'm tired."

"Let us sit down and rest for a while," proposed the tailor.

"I'm thirsty too," said the soldier. "I wish there were a spring of water nearby, or a fruit tree."

"Have this apple," offered the tailor, taking a rosy apple from his pocket.

"Thank you kindly," said the soldier; he took the apple, ate it, and fell asleep.

At that moment the princess came driving along in her coach.

"Is he asleep?" she asked the tailor. "Will you waken him."

The tailor began to shake the lad and to shout in his ear; but he seemed neither to feel nor to hear anything, and slept on.

The lady sighed.

"Let him go home with you tonight," she said to the tailor. "When he awakes, give him this ring and bid him meet me here tomorrow."

"I'll do that," promised the tailor.

The lady drove away. Presently the soldier awoke; it was growing dark now, and he was easily persuaded to go home with the tailor. Next morning the tailor thought he'd better give him the ring and the message, and so he set off again.

"Go you with him," the old wife told her son. "He will be tired and thirsty again. It is not likely he will take another apple from you, but maybe he will taste this pear. And maybe you will win the princess for yourself."

It all happened as she said. Just before they reached the meeting-place the soldier felt tired, and they sat down to rest.

"I'm thirsty too," he complained.

"Have this pear, then," offered the tailor.

"But yesterday the apple I ate put me to sleep, and I did not waken until the princess had gone."

"Och, but that is a foolish thought," the tailor told him. "It just happened yesterday that you were extra tired. The pear will refresh you."

The soldier ate the pear, and of course fell asleep.

"Surely he is not asleep again!" exclaimed the princess when she drove up a minute or two later.

"He is, ma'am. Shall I try to waken him for you?"

"I'll take it kindly if you will."

The tailor shook and shouted, but never a touch or a sound reached the poor soldier's senses until after the lady had driven sadly away. She left a knife with the tailor to give to the soldier, with a message bidding him meet her at the same place next day.

That night the soldier again spent with the tailor. In the morning he was given the knife and the message, and set out once more to meet the princess.

"Go you with him again," the old wife told her son. "It will be no use offering him anything to eat now, for he will not take it. But when you sit down, stick this pin into the back of his coat; he will fall asleep, and the sleep he was in these last two days will be nothing to the one he will be in now."

Again the two men walked on until they came near the meeting-place. This time the soldier said nothing about being thirsty; but when they halted, the tailor stuck the pin into the back of his coat, and he fell into a deep slumber, just as the princess drove up, attended by two servants.

"Is he asleep again?" she asked despairingly.

"Indeed and he is, ma'am," said the tailor.

"Waken him if you can," bade the princess.

The tailor shook the lad violently, he roared in his ear, but without rousing him at all.

"Then we'll take him asleep as he is," said the lady, and told her servants to lift him. They were big, strong fellows, but they could not move him an inch from the ground.

The lady sighed.

"Give him this," she said to the tailor, handing him a gold pin. "But no message, for I will not come again."

When she had driven sadly away and was out of sight, the tailor drew the sleep-making pin from the soldier's coat, and he awoke.

"Has she come?" he asked anxiously.

"She has come and gone; and you are not likely to see her again. She left no message, only gave me this pin to give you. And now you'd better be coming home with me."

"I will not," declared the soldier. "I have gone home with you too often, and I wish I had not. Now I'll be off by myself on my own way, so goodbye to you."

He went on and on, always asking where he might come to the Kingdom of the Green Mountains, but never a one could tell him for never a one had heard of such a realm. One day he came to a house where an old man was thatching the roof with sods of turf, and greeted him courteously.

"You are old, are you not, to be doing such work?" he asked.

"I am old," said the old man, "but my father is older."

"And he is alive and well?"

"He is; and now, where are you going?"

"I am going to the Kingdom of the Green Mountains if I can find the way."

"Never in my long life have I heard of that kingdom, but maybe my father will know," said the old man.

"And where is your father that I may ask him?"

"He is fetching the divots of turf to me, and he will be here in a minute or two; then you can ask him."

Very soon the old man's father came up with a load of turf, and he was very old indeed.

"Faith, you are old," said the soldier in a wondering voice.

"I am that; but my father is older than I," said the old man's father.

"And is he still living?" asked the soldier.

"Sure he is, and why not?"

"Could you tell me now, the way to the Kingdom of the Green Mountains?" asked the soldier politely.

"I have never heard of it, but maybe my father has."

"Where is he?" asked the soldier.

"He is over there, cutting the turf. Come now and ask him."

They found the third old man whose age seemed beyond belief.

"Och, but you are old," exclaimed the lad.

"Old I may be, but my father is older."

"And can you tell me the way to the Kingdom of the Green Mountains?"

"I cannot; but my father is likely to know."

"And where can I find your father?"

"He is out on the hill hunting birds. Wait you, he will be home soon and you can ask him."

This fourth old man—older than the hills, it seemed to the soldier—was, when he came back, as civil as his son, his grandson and his great-grandson had been, but he knew no more than they about the Kingdom of the Green Mountains.

"But I think my father will know," he added kindly.

The soldier who, by this time, was past being amazed, asked where the father might be.

"He is within, in the house; come you in and ask him."

They went in together, and there was an old, old man by the fire; older than can be imagined, as old as the hills or older; so old that he was lying in a cradle.

"Ah, what a great age is on you," said the soldier respectfully.

"Och yes, I've reached a fair age," agreed the ancient.

"And have you heard at all of the Kingdom of the Green Mountains?"

"Faith, and I have not."

That seemed the end of the matter; but the old men were kind, and they were sorry for this lad who seemed to them hardly more than an infant.

"Come with me to the hill tomorrow," said the fowler. "When I blow my whistle all the birds of the air will come flying to me from every kingdom in the wide world; and that way I'll find out for you where the Kingdom of the Green Mountains may be."

The soldier thanked them all from his heart, and spent the night with them in their house, being kindly treated. Next morning he left, with the fowler, for the hill. There the old man blew his whistle, and a flock of birds, the greatest ever seen, came flying to him from every part. Last of all came a great eagle.

"Why are you so late, you sluggard?" asked the old fowler.

"I have had so much farther to fly," pleaded the bird.

"And where are you from?"

"From the Kingdom of the Green Mountains."

"Well, that is good; for here is a lad that wants to go there, so tomorrow you can carry him on your back."

"I'll do that willingly," promised the eagle, "if I am given meat enough."

"You'll have all the food you want," promised the fowler. He dismissed the rest of the birds, the eagle came home with him and the soldier. They were given a good supper, a good breakfast next morning, and a good portion of meat to take with them.

The eagle took the soldier up on her back and flew swift and high. As she flew, she ate her own portion of meat.

"I have eaten all my food," she told the soldier presently. "I am hungry, and growing weak. I must set you down."

"Ah, do not do that," he begged. "I have most of my share left, and you may have it."

That satisfied the eagle for a while, and she flew a long way. Then she said:

"I am hungry again, and growing weak. I must set you down."

"Ah, do not leave me here; bring me at least to the borders of the Kingdom of the Green Mountains."

"I will, if you can give me some meat."

"Alas, I have none left, or I would gladly let you have it."

"You have meat on your own thigh. Let me eat some of that."

The lad thrust his thigh under her beak; she ate, and declared it the sweetest meat she had ever tasted, and she flew on a long way. Then she told him:

"I can carry you no farther, I am so weak with hunger. But if you let me eat from your other thigh I can go on."

He did not much care for the idea, but he put his other thigh beneath her beak, and when she had eaten her fill she flew on swiftly and strongly, saying:

"Now I can reach the Kingdom of the Green Mountains."

Before long, she was swooping down, and she left him on the ground within the borders of the kingdom. Then she flew away. The soldier was thankful to be there, but he felt half-dead from the loss of flesh and blood; he was pitifully lame too, and starving with hunger. But he had a brave heart, and he limped on until he came to the house of the gardener of the King of the Green Mountains. The gardener's wife had pity on him; she brought him in, bathed and bandaged his wounded thighs, gave him food and drink and let him sleep out his weariness. Her skill and kindness healed him, and when he was well and strong again, which was not very long, he took service with the gardener, who was as good-hearted as his wife.

One day the gardener brought the news that the king's daughter was to be married, and that there would be a feast.

"If only I might have a sight of the princess," said the soldier.

"And why wouldn't you?" said the kind woman. "I'll arrange that for you."

She produced a good suit of clothes, saw that he was well-turned out and handsome, and gave him a basket of apples.

"Take that to the princess," she told him, "but give it to her herself, into her own hands, and let none of the servants take it from you."

The soldier thanked her and set off. He came to the palace where he said he had a basket of apples from the gardener's wife for the princess.

One servant after another would have taken it from him, but he refused to give it up.

"I was told to give it into the princess's own hands," he told them. "And I beg you to take me to her."

He was led to the princess's own room. Bowing low, he handed her the basket.

"My thanks to the good wife who sent it," said the princess graciously, "and to yourself for bringing it. And now you will drink a glass of wine."

"Will you drink a glass first?" begged the soldier. She laughed, and drank, and filled the glass again for him.

He bowed low, drank the wine and gave her back the glass—into which he slipped the ring he had kept so carefully. She recognized it.

"Where did you find this ring?"

"Do you remember the soldier you sent to a tailor for a fine suit of clothes?"

"I think I do. But have you further proof?"

"I have this," said the lad, handing her the knife.

"Is that all?"

"No," said the soldier, "there is this besides," and he gave her the gold pin.

"It is all true," declared the princess. "And I am rejoiced to see you."

He had once put his arms round her, but now it was she who put her arms round him with great love.

"This is the husband I have chosen," she told her father the king. "I will have no other."

It was all arranged then; they must have done something handsome for the man the princess was supposed to marry, perhaps found him a fine lady about the court. Anyhow, there was no quarrel, and the soldier went back to tell the gardener and his wife all about it, and the happy ending to his adventures.

"You may be sure," he told them, "that you will never lack anything

I can give you, for you are my true friends and have helped me to win my bride."

There was great rejoicing, and a splendid feast followed the wedding. Then the princess took her husband to the palace where they had first met; the way back was not so long as he had thought. She told him about the two men who had come before her, and had displeased her, and how she had punished them.

"Will you not release them now?" he begged.

This she did willingly. The soldier recognized his old comrades and gave them a kind welcome. He found good places for them, and they were his friends always. But the best friends of all were the good gardener and his kind wife. And they were all very happy.

Habetrot

Meg was as bonny, good and gay a lass as any mother could desire, but in her own mother's eyes she had one fault: she would not spin. She was by no means lazy or sluttish but she hated spinning. If she took up her spindle for half an hour she was bored, and the thread she spun was rough and broken. Any other household task she would do willingly and quickly, and as soon as it was done she would be off to the fields and woods.

"Ye'll never find a man to wed ye," her mother told her. A husband might not demand a dowry in money but it was expected of a bride that she bring to her new home a good plenishing of linen, spun by herself: sheets and table-cloths, shirts for her husband, under-linen for herself. It was a disgrace not to have a well-filled aumbry or cupboard. In those days housewives did not have a weekly laundry; they had enough linen to go on with for months, and then had a tremendous washing and bleaching.

Meg laughed when her mother scolded her. She did not worry her head about finding a husband. No man was worth the dreary task of spinning. So she continued her cheerful, out-of-doors way until one morning her mother said sternly:

"Enough of your gadding about, my lass. You'll sit down and spin these seven hanks of lint before you go out, and you'll have nothing but bread and water until you've finished."

Meg knew she could not escape her task this time. Sitting down with her spindle and what looked to her an immense bundle of lint, she began slowly and clumsily to spin. The day passed, and she had not spun a hank; the next day was no better. Never had time passed so wearily. Meg would sing about her housework as she did when wandering in the fields and woods but over her spinning she was dumb. That night she cried herself to sleep.

She did sleep, however, and woke early in the morning; rose, dressed and went out, taking spindle and flax with her, down to the river. It was a fine, fresh morning, the dew sparkling on the grass, the birds singing in tree and bush: a day for wandering.

As she came down to the river-bank Meg saw a great stone with a hole in it, like a small door. Beside it sat a little woman with a spindle. She looked kind and comely enough except for her mouth which was wide and thick-lipped, the lower lip hanging down to her chin.

"Good day to you," said Meg in her friendly way.

"And good day to you, my lass," said the woman in a thick, mumbling but friendly voice.

"What ails your lips?" asked Meg: a question the little woman did not appear to mind at all.

"That comes from spinning, my dear. Every thread I spin I wet and pull with my lips, and many a thread have I spun."

"So that's what spinning does to you. I hate spinning, but my mother makes me do it," Meg told her.

"Ah well, it's no work for a lass as blythe and bonny as you. Let me have your lint and I'll see what I can do."

Meg very willingly handed over her bundle, and sat down to talk to this good friend whom she told all about the things she liked doing. Presently she began to feel sleepy; the sound of spinning was pleasant when someone else was doing it. Meg fell asleep, but not so soundly that she did not hear, or dream that she heard, the little woman say:

"Habetrot's my name and I'm a spinner like my mother before me and all my sisters."

Then Meg saw, or dreamed that she saw, that Habetrot was no longer there, but through the hole in the stone she could look down into a cave where a group of little women, Habetrot among them, sat busily spinning. Like Habetrot herself they all looked kind and not uncomely, but they all had that ugly, long, thick-lipped mouth. Habetrot seemed to be telling them about Meg and they answered, but all in such mumbling voices that their words could not be made out. Beside each woman lay a pile of flax and on every spindle were lengths of smooth thread. They began singing a sad little song. As far as Meg could make it out they were lamenting their ugly mouths and mumbling speech.

Then she awoke. She had slept all day, it was dusk, and there was no one there but herself; no sound came from the cave; but beside her lay her spindle and seven hanks of thread, perfectly spun, smooth as silk.

"Och, my blessings and my thanks, kind Habetrot," exclaimed Meg.

She gathered up the thread and ran home. Her mother had gone to bed but the kitchen was still warm in the glow from the fire. Hanging from the rafters were seven puddings which the good housewife, Meg's mother, had made that day. Meg was hollow with hunger; she pulled down one pudding, ate it, found it so good that she ate another

—and in not much more than seven minutes had eaten the seven puddings. Then she went to bed and slept.

The first thing her mother saw next morning was the finely spun thread which pleased her so much that she could not be angry about the puddings. Indeed she felt rather proud of a daughter who could eat so many as well as spin so well (or so she thought). She talked to herself about it:

"All that lint spun in three days and never a knot or a break in the thread. Meg that would hardly put her hand to the spindle till I drove her to it. Then back she comes and eats seven puddings. What a lassie! She's welcome to them—I'll be making more."

Thus the good woman talked to herself as she bustled about. It was a fine, sunny morning, the door stood open and the young laird came along. He was a well-set-up, good-looking man with a good name for kindness and pleasant manners. Besides, he had a fine house and lands. Many a girl set her cap at him, many a mother tried to catch him for her daughter, but so far he had seen none that took his fancy.

For a moment he stood listening, with amusement, to the good wife's talk, then he knocked at the door and went in:

"That must be a clever daughter of yours," he said.

"Indeed and she is, and a good lass too," Meg's mother told him proudly.

At that moment, Meg herself appeared, fresh as a rose after her sleep, bright-eyed and smiling. The young laird looked at her, bowed, looked again and fell in love; and there was love on her side too.

Well, there he stayed, talking to Meg and her mother. The good wife asked him to stay to dinner which he did; he teased Meg about her appetite for savoury puddings and she laughed. When he went home he told his mother about his meeting. She knew Meg's mother and thought well of her; Meg, she had heard, was a good and bonny girl but no hand at the spinning. That, her son replied, did not seem to be true. He had seen the thread she had spun in three days and it was perfect. And anyhow, it would not matter whether she could spin or not; his house was already well plenished, and there were maids to do all the spinning that was needed.

Before many days had passed, the laird had asked Meg to marry him and she had happily consented. Her mother was delighted, and his mother, when shown the fine thread, was well pleased. Only Meg was not happy about this. She was an honest lass and had no notion at all of tricking or deceiving her sweetheart, nor had she any intention of learning to spin well. So she told him the whole story.

He laughed and kissed her.

"There's linen enough in my house," he told her, "and I'm not seeking a wife to do the spinning. I like you fine, as you are, my lass."

That was good hearing for a bride.

Next morning the young laird was out early, as usual, and he walked down to the river, thinking about Meg's tale. He saw the stone; it had been moved aside and he could hear voices, and look right down into the cave where the group of women sat spinning. Indeed he walked in and down and spoke to them very pleasantly. They had been singing their sad little song about their looks being so spoiled by their ugly mouths. Now they spoke to the young laird in what he realized was an amiable and friendly manner, although he could hardly make out their words, so mumbling were their voices.

One of them, Habetrot herself, spoke a little better than the others and she told him of her meeting with Meg.

"She's a braw lass and a kind. See that she doesna spoil her bonny mouth by spinning and drawing the thread. There's others that can do the work. Bring a' your lint to us and we'll spin it: linen for your bed, linen to wear, the finest ye'll ever see."

"Thank you; I'll do that. And you'll all come to the wedding," said the bridegroom courteously. "And you'll let me send you cake and wine and anything else you fancy."

"Thank you kindly," said Habetrot. The other women rose and curtsied, smiling at him with kind eyes. He bowed and left them, going straight to tell Meg his adventure.

No bride ever brought finer linen to her husband. The new shirts, the new sheets and table-cloths, Meg's own under-linen, were as fine and soft as silk. It was a grand wedding, the whole countryside came, and the spinners were among the guests of honour at the high table.

Many a time thereafter did Meg leave bundles of flax at the stone beside the river. The women spun all the linen thread to make fine christening robes for her babies, and in return there was always a supply of the best food and drink from the kitchen and larder and cellar of the laird's house. The women used to mumble their thanks which Meg and her husband came more and more to understand. And Meg was free to wander the fields and woods, more cheerfully than ever, for now she had her husband with her, and their bairns.

The Young King of Easaidh Ruadh

The young King of Easaidh Ruadh had newly come to his kingdom,
and he was in high spirits, spending his days in sports and games, his
nights in feasting and music. He liked to play against an opponent,
whether it was at throwing the ball or at chess, or whatever, and to
make a wager, and if he were best pleased at winning he took it in
good part if he lost, and paid the wager cheerfully—which might be a
horse or a hound or a spear or a belt. One day he declared he was going
to challenge a Gruagach or wizard, who lived not far from his palace,
to a game of chess.

"I would not be challenging him, if I were you," said a wise man in
the king's household, to whose advice he sometimes listened.

"But I want to; I must meet him," answered the king.

"Well if you must—then listen to me and take my advice about the
reward you should ask if you win. Ask for the girl with the rough,
brown skin and cropped hair he has in his house."

"I'll do that," promised the king and away he went riding to the house of the Gruagach who came to meet him, and a fierce, ugly-looking character he was, but the king had no fear. He challenged the Gruagach to a game of chess, the winner to name his prize, and the Gruagach agreed. They sat down to play and it was a long game for both were skilled players, but in the end the king won.

"What do you ask as prize?" demanded the Gruagach.

"The girl with the rough brown skin and cropped hair you have in the house," answered the king.

"But why would you be wanting that one? I have twenty girls here in the house, all of them beautiful except that one, and you may take your pick."

"I do not want any of them but her," the king said firmly.

The Gruagach scowled.

"I would like to know who advised you to ask for her," he said, but the king was not telling.

"Well, stand outside the door and I'll send them out and maybe you will change your mind."

The young king stood outside the door and one by one a procession of girls came out, each seeming lovelier than the one before and all of them lovely; nineteen came out, and then the twentieth who was rough and brown of skin, with cropped hair and not at all beautiful.

"That's the one," declared the king. He took her by the hand, led her off, lifted her to the saddle behind him and rode away.

They had not gone far before the girl said, in a very sweet voice: "Will you turn and look at me?"

The king turned and looked and nearly fell off his horse in surprise; for the rough brown lass had become the most beautiful lady he had ever seen, lovelier than any of the nineteen back in the house of the Gruagach.

"I am giving you my heart's thanks and my heart's love," she told him. "You have broken the spell laid upon me and this is my true self. The Gruagach will not be giving you any thanks, for I know too much and I can warn you against him. You had better not be playing any more games with him."

"Indeed and I don't want to," said the king, "now that I have won you."

He carried her joyfully to his palace and there was a great welcome for them; a wedding and a wedding-feast, with the wise man as guest of honour.

The young king lived in bliss with his bride—for a day or two. Then he grew restless.

"I must have another game with the Gruagach," he told the queen.

"I wish you would not," she begged.

"But I must; this once more."

"Well, if you must, good luck go with you. But listen to my counsel. If you win—ask for the shaggy brown filly with the wooden saddle as reward."

"I'll do that," promised the king, and he kissed her and went away.

The Gruagach came out to meet him. "So you've come back?" he shouted.

"I have indeed, and I challenge you to another game," said the king.

"And are you still pleased with the girl you chose?"

"My heart's delight is in her," the king told him.

They sat down to their game and it was a long one, for both played carefully and skilfully. In the end the king won.

"What do you ask as prize this time?" growled the Gruagach.

"The shaggy brown filly with the wooden saddle."

"That's a poor choice. There are horses in my stable far finer than that, with saddles of the best leather and gold."

"It is the shaggy brown filly I choose," declared the king.

The Gruagach did not ask who had advised him; no doubt he knew. He was bound to give what was asked, and the shaggy brown filly was led out. In hope of winning her and riding her home, the king had not brought his own horse, but had walked. Now he mounted the filly and she was off like the wind, or faster, like a flash of light; in no time at all he was home with the queen running to welcome him. They were in bliss together—for a day or two, and then the young king grew restless and said:

"I must go and challenge the Gruagach to another game."

"I pray you, do not go." The queen looked at him beseechingly. "You said you would not go again—the day you brought me here. You have won twice, it is not likely that your luck will hold a third time. Do not go, my love."

"Only this one more game, I promise you faithfully. Win or lose, I will not challenge the Gruagach after this," the king told her solemnly.

"Well, if you must—may luck be with you. I cannot advise you what to ask, if you win. I pray that you may, or that the Gruagach, if he win, may not ask too heavy a reward."

The king went off.

"So you are here again," was the greeting he had from the Gruagach.

"I am here, and I challenge you to a game."

They wasted no more words but sat down to play, a long and difficult game, and this time the Gruagach won.

"What do you ask?" said the king, hoping it might not be too heavy, fearing that it would.

"I bind it upon you, and my curse if you fail," said the Gruagach harshly, "that you bring me the sword of light which belongs to the King of the Oak Windows."

The queen knew as soon as she saw her husband come slowly back to the palace that things had gone badly for him. He told her about the Gruagach's demand.

"It is a sore task indeed," said the queen, "but do not lose heart. I cannot help you myself, but the brown filly will take you. Listen to her, for she will guide you well."

The young king was comforted and slept that night in peace. Early in the morning the queen went with him to the stable and herself put the wooden saddle on the shaggy brown filly. The king embraced her and mounted the filly who went off faster than the wind. By nightfall they were outside the palace of the King of the Oak Windows.

"Listen now to me," said the filly. "The sword of light is there, in the king's own room, inside the window. The king is at dinner. Reach in now and take the sword. It has a knob at the end. Draw it out carefully, do not let it touch the window-frame."

The young King of Easaidh Ruadh reached in at the window, he took the hilt and drew it out, very carefully; but the knob on the end touched the window-frame, and let out a screech.

"We'd better be off," said the filly. "The King of the Oak Windows will be after us, ready to take our lives."

She was off like the wind or faster, like a flash of light, the young king carrying the sword.

"Look behind you," said the filly, "and tell me what you see."

"A troop of horses coming swiftly."

"I am swifter than they," said the filly, and indeed she was.

"Look again," she told the king presently.

"I see some black horses coming very swiftly; and ahead of them one black horse with a white face, swifter than they."

"He is indeed; and his rider is the King of the Oak Windows," the filly told him. "That horse is my brother and he has always been swifter than I. He will soon come up with us. As he passes, the king will turn his head to look at you; then you must cut off his head with the sword."

Even as the filly spoke, the black, white-faced horse came up with them; the King of the Oak Windows turned and glared at the young king, who swept the sword up and cut off his head. It fell on the ground; the black horse stopped, the body fell after the head.

"Dismount me now and mount the black horse," the filly told the young king. "Ride him home and I will follow."

He obeyed, and the black horse carried him home even more swiftly than the filly, but she was not far behind, and they were at the palace by daybreak, and there was the queen running joyfully to welcome them and hear all their adventure.

"I must be off at once to take the sword to the Gruagach," said the king. "And I promise you I'll not go there again."

"Listen now and I'll tell you how to be rid of him," said the queen. "The King of the Oak Windows was his brother, and he will know that you could not have the sword unless you had killed him. Do not give the Gruagach the sword at once. He will ask how you got it; tell him it was because of the knob at the end. He will ask again, and you will still hold the sword. He will stretch up his head to look at it. You will see a mole on his neck. Pierce the mole with the sword, and that will be the end of him."

The king went off, leaving his two good horses in the stable to be fed and groomed. When he came to the house of the Gruagach, that one came to meet him.

"Have you brought the sword of light?" he demanded.

"I have it here," answered the king.

"How did you get it?"

"By the knob on the end."

"How did you do that? Let me see—"

The king held the sword high above his head, the Gruagach stretched his neck to look. The king saw the mole plainly, he swung the sword down and pierced the mole. The Gruagach fell dead, and the young king came joyfully home.

His joy did not last, for he found no joy at the palace, only grief and desolation. His servants were lying bound, in hall and in stable, queen and horses had disappeared.

The servants, when the king released them, told how a great giant had come and taken away the queen and the two horses, the black and the brown. The tracks were still plain and the king set forth, heavy with sorrow, to follow them.

He walked all that day and at nightfall came to the edge of a wood where he saw the ashes of a fire. It seemed good to kindle it again and spend the night in warmth if not in sleep. He gathered sticks and as he was lighting them a dog ran out from the wood and greeted him with kindness and courtesy. The king replied with equal courtesy. The dog said:

"Is it seeking your queen and your horses you are? They were here last night with a great giant, and I am thinking they were not happy to be with him. But do not lose heart. Sit you down in the warmth and I will bring game for our supper."

The dog ran back into the wood, and before long he came again carrying some game in his mouth. The king and he together dressed and roasted it, and ate their supper by the fire in friendship.

"Lie down now, and sleep, for you are weary," said the dog kindly. "I will keep watch until morning."

The king, utterly wearied, fell asleep and slept until daybreak. They roasted the rest of the game, and ate their breakfast together, he and the good dog. Then they blessed each other and parted, the dog bidding the king call upon him if ever he were in need.

The track was still plain and all that day the king followed it. At nightfall he came to a cliff, and there saw the ashes of a fire. Again he found wood for the re-kindling and as he was lighting it a great hawk swooped down beside him and spoke to him kindly. The king replied with courtesy.

"Are you seeking your queen?" the hawk asked. "She and the two horses, the black and the brown, were here last night with a giant, and I do not think they were glad to be with him. But do not lose heart. Sit you there in the warmth while I bring food for our supper."

The hawk flew off and very soon came back with a beakful of duck and blackcock. Together she and the king prepared and roasted them and ate their supper together in peace and friendship.

"Sleep now," said the hawk kindly, "while I keep watch," and the tired king slept until daybreak. Together he and the hawk roasted and ate the rest of the game. They parted then, each blessing the other, while the hawk bade the king call upon her in any need.

Again the track was plain and the king followed it until nightfall which brought him to the bank of a river. There again were the ashes of a fire, and having found wood to kindle it, the king was lighting a flame when an otter rose up out of the river, with kind greeting. The king replied courteously.

"You are seeking your queen and the horses that are with her, I am thinking," said the otter. "They were here last night with a giant, and sad they looked to be with him. But do not lose heart. Sit there in the warmth while I catch a salmon for our supper."

The otter dived into the river and came up with a fine large salmon which she and the king prepared and roasted, and ate their supper together in peace and friendship.

"Sleep you now," said the kind creature, "and I'll keep watch."

The king slept until daybreak; then together he and the otter breakfasted on the rest of the salmon, and parted, each blessing the other.

"I am thinking you are not far from the end of your journey," said the otter. "But if ever you are in need, call me and I will come."

The track led on for a bit, then there were rocks; and the king found a hole in the rock and looking down saw in a deep cave, his queen and his two horses. At one side of the rock there was a narrow path and he went down this to the cave, to the great joy of the queen. It is beyond words to tell of their bliss at being together again, and it was joy for the horses too, who were in a corner of the cave. For a time there was talk of all that had happened; how the giant had come and bound the servants and dragged the queen and the horses away. The king told of the death of the Gruagach, of the sorrow of his home-coming, of his journey and of the kind and blessed creatures who had helped him. The queen prepared food, they ate together, then she said:

"You must be hiding now, for the giant will soon be here." She hid him in the corner where the horses were. Presently with a roaring and a stamping the great giant came in.

"I smell a stranger," he roared.

"It is only the smell of the horses," the queen told him. "What stranger could be coming here?"

The giant went to feed the horses, and they turned on him, kicking him, trampling him. As he limped back to the queen he said:

"It is a good thing that my soul is not in my body, for they would have killed me entirely."

"Thankful I am about that," answered the queen sweetly. "But where is your soul?"

"Do you see that stone by the hearth? My soul is there," the giant told her.

He went to sleep then, and next morning went stamping off.

The king came out from his hiding-place, and there was a happy day for them. Before evening the queen went out of the cave to gather fresh herbs and grass. She washed the stone by the hearth and covered it with the herbs and grass; and then the giant was heard stamping along. The king hid in the corner, the queen welcomed the giant sweetly. Again he went to feed the horses, again they attacked and trampled him.

As he limped back towards the hearth he looked at the stone.

"What have you been doing?" he asked.

"Would I not be adorning the stone where your soul is kept?" said the queen, with a smile.

"Och, but you are the fond one. And my soul not there at all. It is over by the threshold."

The night passed and in the morning the giant went off again. The king came from his hiding-place, there was another day of happiness. Again the queen gathered fresh herbs and grass to scatter upon the threshold which she had washed.

The giant came back at dusk, and went to feed the horses, and again was kicked and trampled. He noticed the herb-strewn threshold.

"What have you been doing here?" he asked.

"Is your soul not there, and would I not be adorning the place where it lies?" answered the queen sweetly.

"Sure, you are the fond one, and it not there at all. But this time I tell you truly. Do you see that great flagstone outside the door? Beneath that is a sheep and in the sheep's belly there is a duck, and in the duck's belly an egg; and in that egg is my soul."

Next morning as soon as the giant was well away, the king came out, and he and the queen raised the flagstone. A sheep leaped out and ran quickly away.

"Oh, if the good dog of the wood were here," said the king, and there the dog was, and off he ran swift as the wind. He caught the sheep and brought it back, and the king cut it open. Out of its belly flew a duck high into the air.

The king and the queen were out of the cave now, running up the path on to the rocks.

"Oh, if my good helper the hawk were here," said the king, and there the hawk was, flying high in the air, swooping down on the duck. She brought the duck down, the king cut it open, and out of the duck's belly rolled an egg—which rolled on over the edge of the rocks into the river.

"Oh for the kind otter," said the king. The otter rose up out of the river, dived again and came up with the egg in her mouth. The queen took the egg, she and the king blessed the three creatures who blessed them in return and departed. They ran back to the cave and just as the giant came stamping back the queen crushed and broke the egg. The giant fell dead.

And all they had to do then was to collect the treasure of gold and silver, stolen treasure which the giant had in the cave; loose the horses, mount them and ride up the path and away. That night they passed with the otter, the next with the hawk, the third with the dog of the wood, in great friendliness and thankfulness, and they parted, each blessing the other. Then they came home to their palace, and any joy that had ever been there was nothing to the joy which welcomed them now, and the joy which remained all their lives.

6

The Black Bull of Norroway

There were three beautiful sisters who lived with their mother. They were not at all rich and they grew tired of being at home. One day the eldest said to her mother:

"Bake me a bannock and roast me a collop, and I'll away to seek my fortune."

The mother baked her a bannock and roasted her a collop or piece of meat, and the girl put them into a bag, and went off to the house of a wise woman, to ask her advice.

"Bide here with me until you see what happens," said the wise woman.

The girl stayed with her that night. All next day she waited and watched, but nothing happened. She stayed another night and another day, and on the third day the wise woman told her:

"Look out at the door."

And there stood a coach and six.

"That's for you," the wise woman said.

The girl got into the coach and drove away. The tale tells no more about her, but it is likely that she was driven to the castle of a knight or a baron who wanted a wife, and so she was married, and that was fine.

The second daughter, not long after that, said to her mother: "Bake me a bannock, mother, and roast me a collop, and I'll away to seek my fortune."

She was given the bannock and the collop, and off she went to the wise woman who bade her stay for a night and a day, or maybe two, and see what might come.

On the third day the wise woman said:

"Look out at the door, now."

There the girl saw a coach and four coming along the road.

"That's for you," the wise woman told her.

The girl got into the coach and was driven away to find her good fortune.

Then it was the turn of the third daughter, who was also the prettiest. She too begged for a bannock and a collop, and went off with her provision to the house of the wise woman. Then she stayed the night and the next night, and on the third day was bidden to look out at the door. No coach was coming along the road; instead there was a great, black bull.

"That's for you," said the wise woman.

Although she was terrified, the girl could not resist. She was lifted on to the back of the bull and away he went at a great pace, carrying her far from the place she knew. The poor lass was frightened and bewildered and soon she felt tired and hungry too. Then the bull spoke to her, in a deep, kind voice:

"Take food out of my right ear and drink out of my left ear. Eat and drink and be satisfied and put back what you do not need."

The girl found food in his right ear, drink in his left ear, ate and drank all she wanted, and was refreshed and comforted. Her fear began to leave her. On they went, and at nightfall came to a park, and within the park a fine large house.

"Here we bide for the night," the bull told her, in his deep voice. "It is the house of my eldest brother."

He carried her to the door where kind people came to welcome her and lead her in, while the bull went to pasture in the park.

She was taken to a warm room, given a bath, supper, and put to bed where she slept peacefully all night long. In the morning the bull came for her and she was lifted on to his back. Before she left, the people of the house gave her a beautiful apple, bidding her not touch it unless she was in sore need.

That second day was like the first, except that the lass had no longer any fear. At nightfall they came to a park, and within it a fine large house.

"That is the house of my second brother," said the bull, "and here we are to bide the night."

Here too the girl found a kind welcome, with food and rest, and the bull went to pasture in the park. In the morning, before she left, she was given a beautiful pear.

"Do not touch or break it," they told her, "unless you are in desperate need."

The third day was like the first and the second, the girl enjoying her journey now, without a whiff of fear. Indeed she was beginning to love the strong, gentle bull. The third night they came to a park and another fine house within it.

"This is the house of my youngest brother," the bull told her, "and here we bide the night."

And there was a third night of kindly welcome and good rest. In the morning there was a parting gift of a beautiful plum, with the same warning: not to touch it unless she were in sore need.

This day brought no long journey. As the bull carried her off he told her in his kind grave voice:

"Today I must fight with the devil. I am taking you to a glen where you must wait, until the fight is over. If I have lost, everything will turn red; if I have won, everything will turn blue."

Presently they came to a hidden glen where he bade her sit down.

"Be very still. You will see nothing until the fight is over. Do not stir hand or foot, for if you do, you too will become invisible and I shall not be able to find you when I come back."

The girl obediently sat down, very still, and the bull went away. She waited quietly, hearing nothing, seeing nothing. Then suddenly the glen was filled with a clear blue light. That, she knew, meant victory for the bull. In her relief she moved a little; a very little, only lifting one foot and crossing it over the other, but that was enough to make her invisible to the bull when he came seeking her.

The poor lass waited and waited, first in hope, then in despair. At last she wandered away, grieving, trying to find him; sure, now, that he was a brave knight under a spell and the spell now broken. But another had been laid upon her by her moving.

A long, long way she wandered until she came to the foot of a high mountain of glass, so smooth and slippery that she could not set foot upon it. As she walked round it, hoping to find a foothold, she came to a smith's house where she begged for help. The smith told her that if she would serve him for seven years, he would make her a pair of iron shoes, with spikes, in which she could safely climb the glass mountain.

For seven years she served him faithfully, and at the end he said:

"Here is your fee, and may good luck go with you," and gave her a pair of iron shoes, with spikes.

With these on her feet she climbed the glass mountain and at the top found a house where a washerwoman lived with her daughter. She begged food and shelter; they brought her in and offered her work to do. A young knight, they told her, had come to them bringing his blood-stained shirt to wash. He had been sorely wounded in a fight and the stains were deep.

"He said he would marry the woman who washed his shirt clean."

The woman and her daughter had washed and scrubbed, boiled and bleached the shirt, but the stains would not come out.

"Let me try," begged the wandering girl, and they gave her the shirt. When she had washed it, every stain had come out, and the linen was white as snow.

"That's fine," said the washerwoman to her daughter. "The knight will be pleased when he comes to fetch it."

"Aye, but he will marry that lass and we don't want that," said the daughter.

"Indeed he will not. He will marry you. Don't I know how to take care of that?" her mother assured her.

So when the knight came back, they sent the poor wandering girl out of the way, and told him that the daughter had washed his shirt clean. A promise must be kept. The knight knew that he must marry the one who had washed his shirt, though he did not at all want to marry the washerwoman's daughter.

Now the girl had had a glimpse of him, and she knew in her heart, without telling, that he was her true love who had been spell-bound and set free, and whom she had lost, there in the deep glen. She was nearly heart-broken, until she remembered the gift of the apple. This was truly a moment of sore need and she broke the apple, to find it full of jewels.

"Look," she said to the washerwoman's daughter, "I will give you these jewels as a wedding gift if you will let me watch tonight by your bridegroom's bed."

The daughter did not like that idea, but her mother was looking at her and nodding, so she agreed.

"I'll see to that," her mother assured her.

That night she brought the young man a cup of heavily drugged wine. He drank it and fell so sound asleep that he heard nothing, although his true love, the poor wandering girl, sat by his bed all night, singing:

> "Seven long years I served for thee,
> The glassy hill I clomb for thee,
> The bloody sark I wrang for thee.
> Wilt thou not waken and turn to me?"

Next day she took the pear that had been given her, for now she was truly in need again. When she broke it, she found it full of jewels even finer than those in the apple.

"These too I will give you," she told the washerwoman's daughter, "if you will let me sit this night by your bridegroom's bed."

To this daughter readily consented, knowing what would happen. Again the knight was given drugged wine; again he slept so heavily that he did not hear his true love singing her sad song:

> "Seven long years I served for thee,
> The glassy hill I clomb for thee,
> The bloody sark I wrang for thee.
> Wilt thou not waken and turn to me?"

If he did not hear, however, his squire did. The women had forgotten him. He awoke and listened, and in the morning asked the knight if he had not been wakened by the sad song and a voice of weeping. This made the bridegroom wonder and think and begin to remember something.

That day the poor girl took out her last treasure, the plum. Her need was desperate now, for if she could not waken her love, there would be no further chance. He would marry the washer-woman's daughter. The plum held jewels even finer and richer than had the apple and the pear.

"These are for you," the girl told the washerwoman's daughter, "if you will let me watch this night also by your bridegroom."

"That indeed I will," said the other, laughing and clutching the jewels. She went off gleefully to tell her mother who brought another cup of drugged wine to the knight. But this time he was aware of some mischief. He pretended to taste the wine.

"It tastes harsh," he said. "Will you bring me some honey to sweeten it."

The washerwoman went off to fetch the honey. He poured the wine out of the window, and when the woman came back, he had set down the cup and was nodding drowsily.

"So he's drunk it as it was," the woman thought, and left him.

When his true love came he was lying as if asleep. She sat by his bed and began singing her sad song, more sadly than ever for now she had little hope of awakening him:

> "Seven long years I served for thee,
> The glassy hill I clomb for thee,
> The bloody sark I wrang for thee.
> Wilt thou not waken and turn to me?"

And now he heard and he was awake; he rose and took his true love in his arms. They spent the night telling each other of all they had gone through, for the knight had sought her long and despairingly. Now they were together and could ride away.

In the morning the washerwoman and her daughter found them together. Some say that the knight slew them both for their treachery, but others say, and it is more likely, that he laughed and left them raging at him and his true love and at each other; which did not help them at all and they may be raging still.

As for the knight and his bride, they rode swiftly and happily to the house of one of his brothers, there to be welcomed and feasted and tell of their adventures. The bride was given a fine gown for her wedding and many other gifts. Then they rode on to the other brother's house, and to the third, always to the most joyful of welcomes. Finally they came to the bride's mother whose heart was full of joy and thankfulness. They lived together happily always, and they may very well be living contentedly until this day.

7

Thomas the Rhymer

Thomas Learmont, laird of Ercildoune, liked to wander about the green countryside of the Borders, a land of hills and glens, rivers and burns and waters. He would make his rhymes and songs as he walked, then sit down by the water or under a tree to play a tune on his harp which he always carried with him: a small harp which could be slung over his shoulder.

One day he was sitting under the Eildon Tree by Huntlie Burn playing a tune which held the ripple and running of a Border stream in it, the lilt of a blackbird and something else besides, something old and strange and magic. How it had come to him he could not tell. As he sat there he looked up and saw a ferlie or marvel. A lady came riding down the water-side; she rode a milk-white horse with a bridle of silver and green, and she was dressed in silk as green as grass with a golden girdle and a circlet of gold upon her head. The bells on the bridle jingled as she rode.

Thomas thought he had never seen so fair a lady. He rose, swept off his hat and bowed low. Surely, he thought, this was no mortal lady. Dropping on one knee he hailed her reverently as the Queen of Heaven. The lady laughed, and her laugh, though clear as the silver bells, was not altogether good to hear. There was coldness in it.

"No, no, Thomas" (how did she know his name?), "I am not the Queen of Heaven. That name is not mine. I am but the Queen of Elfland and I have come to visit you, for I know your fame as a harper and rhymer. Now, I beg you, play me a tune and sing to your playing."

Thomas played the air he had been trying on his harp when he saw the lady. She listened with delight.

"I owe you a fee for that," she said. "What will you have as a reward?"

"I would have a kiss," replied Thomas gallantly.

The queen laughed.

"Thomas, if you dare to kiss my lips, I am sure of your body. It will belong to me."

"That fate will not daunton me," declared the Rhymer, and he kissed her.

"Now, Thomas, you are mine and must come with me, and stay with me and serve me for seven years."

Thomas knew too much about fairy law and fairy power to resist. He mounted behind the queen on her milk-white steed and they rode away, far and fast; faster than the wind, the swiftest wind could not overtake them. They rode far beyond Huntlie Burn, beyond Ercildoune and Leader Water, beyond Tweed and all the Border waters until they came to a wild and desolate place unlike all the valleys and pastures that Thomas knew, wilder than the hills, more desolate than any bleak moorland he had seen. The lady reined in her horse.

"Here we dismount, Thomas. And now lie down with your head on my lap and I shall show you three ferlies."

Thomas obeyed. Looking over the desolate land he saw three roads. One was rough, stony and narrow with thorns growing beside it.

"That," the queen told him, "is the way of righteousness, and few walk there."

Thomas had indeed heard that often in church, from the priest.

The second road was wide and smooth, bordered with flowers, leading through a green meadow; a very pleasant road.

"That is the way to hell, though many think it the way to heaven. Many walk there."

The third road was a winding one by a hillside, leading through bracken and brambles.

"And that is the way to my kingdom, to fair Elfhame. That is the way you and I must ride," said the queen. "And when you come there you must be silent for seven years; you must serve me for all that time, and if you speak one word you will be my captive for ever, and never return to your own country."

They mounted horse again and rode on; on and on through a strange land, through rivers of blood, for all the blood shed upon earth runs through the streams of that country. They saw neither sun nor moon nor stars, but rode through mirk night. There was no sound of human speech or of birdsong, only the far-off roaring of the sea.

At last they came to a fair green garden and orchard, where apple trees grew laden with bright fruit. The queen plucked an apple and gave it to Thomas.

"Take that for fee, Thomas. It will give you the tongue that cannot lie, and you will be True Thomas."

"My tongue is my own," protested Thomas. "With such a gift how could I bargain at market, or talk freely to any man, or make love to any lady?"

"Hold your peace, True Thomas. It must be as I say. And now, keep silence for seven years."

So they came to Elfhame, a country which some say is almost as lovely as Paradise; but others that it is a place of deception, of shadows and illusion where the people are hollow and shadowy, and what appears to be gold turns to dry twigs and withered leaves. However that may be, Thomas must bide there for seven years. He was given a coat of fine green cloth, and shoes of velvet green as grass. In silence he served the queen and of that service we know nothing for he never spoke of it after his return. But it is likely that he played his harp often, for her pleasure and that her court danced to his harping.

> "And till seven years were gane and past,
> True Thomas on earth was never seen."

The seven years ended. He was free to return to his own country, to Ercildoune. He came quietly at dusk, slipping in among his family, taking his place by the fire. His wife who had waited patiently and sorrowfully for him, was glad, his older children knew him—but the baby had long grown out of babyhood and had no memory of him at all. He was dearly cherished, dearly welcome, yet there was a shadow about all the rejoicing. He looked grave, remote, his voice had changed; it was slow and very quiet as if he were trying to remember how to speak. None asked where he had been and he did not tell.

Gradually he took up his old way of life, mingling with his neighbours, playing his harp at their feasts, singing songs and playing tunes lovelier than any they had ever heard. He was found always to speak the truth, in great things and small and so was given his other name of True Thomas. Sometimes he made prophecies which are still remembered.

One was about his own house:

> "The hare shall kittle on my hearth-stane
> And there never will be a Laird Learmont again."

Time passed and people forgot the strange disappearance and return of Thomas of Ercildoune. But he did not forget, and the summons came again.

There was a feast in his tower; many lords and ladies gathered for music and dancing. They drank the good red wine and listened to Thomas as he played his harp and sang of the doings of King Arthur (who, some say, sleeps with his knights inside the Eildon Hills), sang so sweetly and movingly that the ladies wept and even some of the tough warriors had tears in their eyes.

That night one of them, Lord Douglas, lay wakeful with some foreboding in his mind. Hearing footsteps, he rose and looked out. He saw a hart and a milk-white hind come from the forest, pacing towards the tower. Then Thomas came out carrying his harp slung from his shoulder, and followed them. Once he turned to look at his house and bid farewell. Then, following the fairy deer sent to summon him, he departed, no man could tell where, though many guessed. He came no more to Ercildoune.

But one tale tells that he did come again to the Borders, long afterwards, again released from Elfhame; not to his own home where now the hare kittled on the bare hearth-stane but to a monastery on Tweedside, and there lived for a time in silence and peace and prayer, until he ended his days in holiness.

8

The Lady and the Elf-Knight

Lady Isabel sat at her window sewing a fine seam. She was young and beautiful, the cherished daughter of her noble parents but she was discontented, bored, and rather sorry for herself. Only the day before her sister had been married and she was younger than Lady Isabel who thought she should have been the bride and not merely the bridesmaid.

Suddenly there sounded, sweet and clear, the note of a horn. From her window high in a tower of her father's castle Lady Isabel could see on the hillside a knight who was blowing his horn—to east and west, north and south. He was a stranger and from his look of extreme charm, from his green cloak and from the sound of his horn, she felt sure he was from Elfland.

The horn sounded again, clear, sweet and compelling: "I wish I had that horn to keep, and I wish that knight were here with me in my bower," said Lady Isabel to herself. Even as she spoke the knight was there, in his green cloak, holding his horn and bowing courteously.

Lady Isabel looked at him lovingly and would have embraced him.

"Lady, you are too young. You would not be happy if I married you."

"I am not too young," retorted Lady Isabel indignantly. "My sister who was married yesterday is younger than I."

"Well," said the elf-knight, "if you would marry me you must first do me a service."

"And what must I do?"

"You must make me a shirt without any cut or hem, having shaped it without scissors or knife, sewn it without needle or thread; then you must wash it in a well where no drop or dew or rain has fallen and dry it on a thorn-bush that never bore bud since Adam was born."

Lady Isabel looked at him with a smile.

"Very well; but in return you must do me a service."

"What must I do?"

"You must give my father an acre of land between the sea and the shore; this you must plough with your horn and sow with peppercorn. Then you shall harrow it with one harrow-blade and shear it with a horse-bone. The corn you must stack in that mouse-hole in the corner, then thresh it in the sole of your shoe, winnow it in your hand and store it in your glove. And then you shall bring it clean and dry over the sea. Will you do that? When you have done it, you shall have your shirt."

"Then I will not come again to you, fair lady, or leave my own wife and bairns."

"And I will not give you my love and my maidenhood, Sir Elfin Knight. You may go and take with you your elfin horn, and blow it upon the hillside again or wherever you will."

Whuppity Stourie

There was a poor woman once, a widow whose husband had been killed in the wars. She was known as The Goodwife of Kittlerumpit and she was a sensible woman who made the best of things, brave too and quick-witted. She had one child, a baby and she lived in a wee house, only a *but-and-ben* (which means an outer and inner room) at the top of a brae and at the edge of a wood. She kept a pig and looked after it well; the pig was about to farrow which would mean having piglets to sell at the market and perhaps one to keep, and money to buy food and clothes for her bairn and herself.

So, it was with dismay that one morning, going to the pig-sty with a bucket of food, she found the poor pig lying on its back squealing and grunting in pain: a very sick pig. What could she do, poor woman? If the pig died there would be no piglets to take to market, no money, no warm clothes and not much food. The Goodwife sat down and cried. That did not help much, and very soon she was on her feet again, going back to her cottage to feed her baby, when she saw, coming up the brae, a tiny woman, no bigger than a young child, but with a face not at all childlike. The woman was dressed in green, with a white apron, a black cloak, and a tall, peaked black hat.

"Good day to you, ma'am," said our Goodwife, dropping a curtsy to the little green woman. "Will your leddyship listen kindly to me? I am sair troubled and helpless. My gude man is deid, I've a wee bairn to feed and clothe, and now the pig is like to die that was to have farrowed in a day or two. What am I to do?"

"Do you think I care for your troubles?" said the fairy woman, for that is what she was. "I've mair to do than that. But I'll make a bargain with you. If I cure your pig, as well I know I can, will you give me what I ask in payment? I shall not be asking for money."

"Whatever you ask, if I have it I shall give it to you," promised the Goodwife.

Then the fairy woman walked into the pig-sty, looked at the pig rolling and grunting in pain, and muttered something which sounded like this:

"Pitter-patter, haly water,"
and taking a small bottle from her pocket sprinkled a few drops on the pig's snout. The creature grunted again, rolled over, got up and waddled to the trough where, with loud noises, it began tucking into the mash.

"Thank you and bless you, my lady," said the Goodwife, dropping on her knees and trying to kiss the hem of the fairy woman's green gown.

"Up with you, you daft wife. I've no use for kissing and blessing. I've done my part and you maun do yours. We made a bargain, you maun keep it. The payment I ask is your bairn."

The poor mother set up a heart-broken sobbing and wailing.

"Och, my leddy, gracious leddy, not my bairn, my ain wee bairn. Ask onything else ye like, ony service; I'll work my fingers to the bone for you."

"I have nae need of any service the likes of you can do. There's naething of yours I want—only your bairn whom you are bound to give me, so away and fetch him. I've kept my side o' the bargain. And nae mair o' your lamenting. I can promise you the bairn will be well cared for. But I'll tell you this. By our laws I canna take him until the third day from now, and I canna take him at a' if you can say my name. But that's no' likely," and she laughed in a way not pleasant to hear. With a swirl of her green gown and her black cloak she was off, down the brae out of sight.

The poor mother wept, hugging her wee son to her breast, as if she would never let him go. All that night she held him in her arms and all the next day. She could not sleep for grief, and for fear that the fairy woman might come and take him away.

On the second day she went out, carrying the sleeping baby, out into the wood, farther in than she had ever gone before, hardly knowing why, only seeking a little peace. At the heart of the wood she found a spring, and sitting by it with a spinning-wheel, a tiny woman in a green gown, a white apron, a black cloak and tall black hat. The mother recognized the fairy, who did not see her for the mother was walking very softly, very carefully, so as not to waken her baby. She walked on the soft grass without treading on any fallen twig.

As the spinning-wheel turned and whirred, the spinner sang softly to herself. The Goodwife crept nearer, hidden by the thick trees. She stood and listened, and this is the song she heard:

"Little kens the gudewife at hame
That Whuppity Stourie is my name."

And she laughed with a sound that was far from good to hear.

Softly, carefully the mother drew back, praying that her child might not waken. He slept peacefully on. Softly, swiftly she went back through the wood, her heart full of prayer and thankfulness; came safely home and shut the door on her baby and herself. That night she slept well.

Next morning, the third day, she was ready for the fairy woman as she came up the brae in her green gown and white apron, her black cloak and tall, peaked black hat.

"Well, Gudewife, I'm here for my fee. Ye maun keep the bargain."

"Must I so, Whuppity Stourie?" said the Goodwife, very politely, curtsying as she spoke.

With a skirl of rage and a wild swirl of green and black skirts the fairy woman was off down the brae and out of sight, whipping up the dust or stour as she whirled away. And that was the last sight and sound of her.

The Goodwife of Kittlerumpit went back to her fireside. She fed her baby and sang to him and he smiled and chuckled. In a day or two the pig farrowed and the piglets were sold at market, all but one the Goodwife kept for herself. They fetched a good price and she was able to buy warm clothes and good food for her bairn and herself. From that day they both began to thrive and the baby grew into a fine laddie. But never again did the wife ask help from The Other People.

10

The Queen of Elfland's Nurse

"I heard a cow low, and a bonnie cow lo
  And a cow low doun in yon glen;
Lang, lang will my young son greet
  Or his mither bid him come ben.

"I heard a cow low, and a bonnie cow low,
  And a cow low doun in yon fauld;
Lang, lang will my young son greet
  Or his mither tak' him frae cauld."

Kirsty sat by the cradle of her fairy-nursling and sang her sad little song. It had a sweet melody and the elfin baby slept peacefully. The queen his mother was lying in her bed in her bower, and it was for her that Kirsty sang the song, praying that it would reach her heart.

Never before had Kirsty sung a sad lullaby. To her own baby son she had sung happy songs and he had fallen asleep. But one day—was it seven days ago or seven weeks?—a strange woman had come to the door begging milk and food for her sick child. She looked very poor and Kirsty had gladly brought her in, made her sit by the fire, brought food and milk.

"I wish my son were like yours," the woman said, looking at wee Dougal asleep, rosy and bonny. "He is a frail bit thing, he has a fever I think, I have so little to give him and little skill in nursing. Would you not come and look at him? It is but a step or two from here. You have skill, I can see; you will tell me what to do and then come back to your own baby."

Kirsty could not resist that. She had indeed a knowledge of nursing, from her mother and grandmother; a neighbour often came to ask her advice. The woman must be a wandering beggar, though she looked clean and decent. It would not take long; besides, Kirsty's younger sister was about the place; she would keep an eye on wee Dougal and on the kail-pot simmering on the hearth.

So Kirsty went off with her guest, who as soon as they came into the wood beyond the house became royal in look, with a strange alluring beauty; instead of a ragged gown and shawl she wore shimmering green silk and a velvet cloak, and a veil delicate as sea-foam. Then Kirsty knew that this was no mortal woman but one of elfin kind, perhaps the queen herself, for she wore a crown of pearls and opals that shimmered like moonlight. And Kirsty was afraid, although the lady smiled on her very kindly and spoke gently in a voice that would lure your heart away: yet there was a coldness about both smile and voice, something not evil or cruel but strange and remote.

"Kirsty, you are coming with me to my kingdom and my palace. You will be the most honoured guest. My young son needs you. Come."

She took Kirsty by the hand and drew her along a green grassy path. A light mist hung about and above them with a pale gleam more of moonlight than of sun, although it was barely noontide. Through the dimness came a milk-white horse saddled and bridled in green, led by a page on a grey horse also saddled in green, and the page wore a grass-green cloak.

"I am not dressed to go to court," Kirsty managed to say.

"That does not matter. You shall have all the dresses, all the fine linen you desire; everything is ready for you. Now, mount behind me," commanded the fairy woman.

The page had dismounted; he lifted the queen on to her white horse, and lifted Kirsty behind her, then mounted his own grey horse again and off they rode, through the wood over a wide plain. It was all so near home, yet so unfamiliar. The queen pointed with her riding-whip of soft green leather with handle of gold:

"There is the road to hell, that flowery path where so many go; and there"—she pointed to a steep and narrow way, rough with stones— "is the way to heaven which few care to follow. But we are riding on the way to fair Elfland and soon we shall be there."

Kirsty hoped in her kind heart that those who had set forth on the way to hell might yet be brought back. The steep road to heaven had been walked by her own grandmother who had been so good and loving; she had died not long before, just after the birth of Kirsty's wee son, whom she had held in her arms and blessed.

Kirsty tried to think of that, but her mind seemed to be clouded, like the road, by a drifting mist. They were riding swiftly, swifter than the wind, the horses were sure of foot, and soon they came out of the mist into a wide green flowery place in the middle of which stood the queen's palace. It was more splendid than any house Kirsty had ever seen, beyond even the castle of the Earl and Countess where Kirsty had been a maid before she married Angus. Her mother and grand-mother had served there too, each in her time and Kirsty's elder sister Jean was there now, as nurse to the baby son and heir. It was a grand castle, with a great hall panelled with carved wood and the Countess's room was hung with tapestries and curtained with silk. But that was nothing compared with the beauty of the fairy palace into which Kirsty was now led. It was full of glimmering, many-coloured lights; there were innumerable servants here, more than at the castle, and one of them, a pleasant woman, led Kirsty to the nursery where the elf-child lay in his cradle, the fairest baby she had ever seen, bonnier, she had to admit, than her own darling wee Dougal and than the little lordly boy at the castle, and both of these were fine bairns. The elfin child had hair like fine-spun gold, a skin like rose-petals, red and white, eyes as bright and green as emeralds—his mother's eyes. He was crying a little and Kirsty instinctively took him into her arms, where he snuggled down, and ceased to cry and fell asleep. And how could she resist that? The queen stood smiling at her, and bade her lay the baby again in his cradle, and then follow the waiting woman, who led her into her own room as it was to be, next door. And Kirsty gasped at the beauty and luxury she found there, beyond anything in her lady's rooms at the castle; a carpet soft as moss, curtains of silk, a bed of carved wood with curtains and covers embroidered with bright flowers. The elfin attendant brought her warm scented water, smelling of herbs and flowers, to wash in, pouring it into a great silver basin, and helped her to change into some of the fine linen underwear, soft as silk, and one of the gay silk gowns that hung in the cupboard. Another fairy servant brought food and wine more delicious than any she had ever tasted, even at the christening feast of the son and heir of the Earl and Countess at the castle, and they had a grand cook there. Then she went back to the nursery to sit by the elfin baby in his cradle and sing to him.

So it began and so it continued—for days, for weeks? Kirsty could not tell. Time seemed to melt and flow away like water. Sometimes she was afraid; she had heard of those who were taken into Elfhame and came home again after, so it seemed to them, a night and a day; but they had found they had been absent for years, and sometimes there was none to remember them.

Had it not been for that dark shadow of fear, and for the drifting mist—like forgetfulness (but never complete oblivion)—Kirsty might have been well content. Her work was light: only to nurse and dress and feed her nursling, to sit by him, to sing him to sleep. Often she took him into the garden and orchard where flowers grew of a brightness and fragrance she had never imagined, and fruit grew for the gathering: all kinds of fruit, such as she had gathered on earth in its season: strawberries and raspberries, apples, plums and pears, but all of a sweetness she had never tasted before; and others more exotic: oranges and peaches and purple grapes.

Everyone treated her with great friendliness and courtesy, as a most honoured guest, and the queen was unfailingly gracious. Her nursling was a joy; he loved her lullabies—and so did many in the household, children and grown ups too. Kirsty had a good store of cradle songs; and one night she began singing one her grandmother had often sung to her, one about Saint Bride of the Isles, who, as legend tells, was nurse to the Christ Child.

> "Saint Bride the herd-maiden
> Was taken, they say,
> To nurse the Lord Jesus
> Asleep in the hay.
>
> She wrapped in her mantle
> Blue, blue as the sea
> About her own islands,
> The Christ Child so wee.

And afterwards, ever
(They tell in the isles),
She cherished the babies
With fondling and smiles;

And sang as she nursed them:

"Who holds you but she
Who held the Lord Jesu
Asleep on her knee!"

At the first mention of the Holy Name the elf child trembled; at the next, he cried. The queen came in, she too trembling and cold, with an awful look on her face.

"Not that song," she commanded.

And Kirsty did not sing it again though she often thought of it, dimly, not clearly—and she found it difficult to say her prayers. It was as if a cloud of sleep came over her although she was not tired. Her thoughts were confused, yet she never forgot altogether to make her devotions; it might be only an Our Father, a Hail Mary. Sometimes, too, when she tried to pray there would be the sound, very sweet, clear and alluring, of fairy music. But always she thought a holy thought and said a holy word or two. Then her memory became clearer. She heard sounds other than the fairy voices in the palaces and the fairy music. One day she heard a very homely sound that she used to hear every day and many times a day at home. And so she sang her own sad little song:

"I heard a cow low, a bonnie cow low,
    And a cow low doun in the glen;
Lang, lang will my young son greet
    Or his mother bid him come ben."

She remembered suddenly how one day she had found wee Dougal crying lustily, scarlet in the face, when she came in from the byre where she had been milking the cow; but as soon as she took him in her arms he was quiet and happy and fell asleep. Her elfin-nursling seemed to like this song, for he was awake, but lay smiling in his cradle. Kirsty sang on:

> "I heard a cow low, a bonnie cow low,
>   And a cow low doun in the fauld;
> Lang, lang may my young son greet
>   Or his mither tak' him frae cauld."

The tears were in her eyes as she remembered how she had warmed her baby by the fire, wrapping him in a shawl. The elf child was asleep now, but in her room beyond the queen was awake.

"What ails you, Kirsty? What do you lack? Tell me, and you shall have it."

"I lack nothing, my lady but my own wee bairn who needs me, and my man Angus."

"But my babe needs you too. Bide with him, Kirsty, bide a while yet, then you can go."

But Kirsty would not be comforted. The queen drew her on to talk.

"Tell me, Kirsty, what was it like at the castle? Is he a fine bairn, the Earl's heir?"

"He is that," said Kirsty proudly. "And my own sister Jean is his nurse."

"And are they kind to her?"

"Och, my lady Countess is kindness itself to all her house; but to none kinder than to her dear bairn's nurse."

And Kirsty told the queen some of the gentle ways of the Countess:

of all the gifts made to Jean besides her good wages; gifts of clothes and food, gifts to take home to her own children. It had always been like that.

"I will give you more than all your sister has ever been given: pearls to wear on your neck, rings to wear on your fingers and in your ears, a chain of gold, a bag of golden guineas to buy another cow, to build a better house, to buy Angus your husband a new fiddle."

Now, how did she know, that wily and beguiling queen, that Angus desired above all things a new fiddle? His was not a very good one; he played well, though sometimes he made a mistake and sometimes scraped a bit though that was maybe the fault of the fiddle. Kirsty was keeping a secret hoard from the money she made from selling butter and cheese and eggs, but it was still long before she could buy a fiddle.

"Bide with my bairn," the queen went on in her sweet, wheedling voice, "until he can toddle beside you, holding your hand; then you may go with many gifts."

But by that time, Kirsty thought, her own baby would be walking, and she not there to hold his hand. He might even be—but she dared not think of this—a great tall lad, even a man, for fairy time cannot be measured by mortal time.

The mists were clearing from her mind; she saw too clearly for her comfort; she remembered as vividly as if she saw and heard them there, beside her, the faces of husband and child, her sisters, the folk she knew. She heard their voices, heard the lowing of her cow. She heard Angus play his fiddle. And she could bear her exile no longer. She grew pale and thin and weak, her voice sank to a whisper, she could no longer sing.

Faithful though she tried to be in all her duties towards her nursling she was no longer of any use as a nurse, and the queen bade her depart. She dismissed her kindly, and gave her good wages: a bag of gold, a flask of wine and food for the journey. And Kirsty set forth on her way.

It was hard going; the road was rough with stones, a mist drifted about. She had travelled so swiftly before, riding behind the queen on her milk-white horse. Now she stumbled along. On one side, she knew, lay the road to hell from which the mist lifted to show a broad green path bordered by flowers, bright in unearthly light; but there was no allurement there for Kirsty, a good Christian lass. As for the steep and narrow way to heaven she hoped, humbly, she might one day be worthy to walk there. The queen had said that few went by it, but Kirsty could think of many: not only the blessed saints but humble folk, her own dear grandmother, she felt sure, among them. Her grandmother had known grief and pain but never lost courage or kindness; the most loving woman Kirsty had ever known and she had left her blessing with her baby. Might she not help Kirsty now?

There was music in the air; the alluring elfin music, which, if she listened to it, could draw her back; there was the voice of the queen, sweet and plaintive, begging her to come, and still more appealing the voice of her elfin-nursling. But Kirsty walked steadily on. She began to be hungry and thirsty and longed to eat some of the food and drink some of the wine that the queen had given her, but something held her back; memories of those who had eaten fairy food and found themselves returning to earth after a hundred years. Perhaps a hundred years had already passed, for she had, of necessity, eaten and drunk in Elfland. To save herself from temptation and to lighten her burden she threw the food away, poured out the wine, laid the empty flask down. There was still the bag of gold—but that was not for herself, it was for Angus, to buy him a new fiddle.

The music was dying away; she heard, very faintly, another song; the voice grew clear and stronger. Surely it was that of her grandmother who had been a sweet singer? And this was no elfin song, for it uttered the Holy Name and praised Our Lord.

The mist was clearing, the road was smoother, she could walk swiftly. There were other sounds, now, other voices: the lowing of a cow; the cry of a baby—and this was no elfin child it was a human one, and very indignant—the cry of a baby demanding his mother, demanding attention, demanding food, and determined to keep on crying until he had what he wanted.

Music sounded: a tune on the fiddle, and that was no fairy music, it was Angus playing (and at this moment scraping) his old fiddle, and—oh! he always made that mistake, though most of the time he played very well. It was one of his and her favourite tunes, and wee Dougal liked it too.

The baby went on yelling and this was the cry of a small—but tough—infant, not of a child of seven or so running about. The music stopped; she heard Angus's voice:

"Kirsty, lass, where are you? Wheesht, laddie, your mother is coming."

Kirsty ran, and came on to the green in front of the cottage. Angus stood there, and Dougal lay on a plaid on the grass.

"Wheesht, I tell you. Och, here ye are lass, I'm glad to see you."

Angus gave her a hug and a kiss. "Where ha'e ye been? The bairn needs ye sair. Naething I can do will please him, your mither has tried and your sisters but he wants you. And so do I."

Kirsty ran to her son, picked him up and cuddled him; he was scarlet in the face, but now he subsided, and smiled at her. The bag of gold had dropped from her arm. Angus picked it up.

"Will you open it?" said Kirsty. "It's for you."

Angus opened it and laughed. The bag was full of leaves. "Thank ye kindly, my lass, I ken well ye meant it kindly and I ken whaur ye've been these seven days. I heard about that beggar wife and I ken fine how she lured you awa'. Come awa' into the hoose, my lass; it's a' as ye left it, and I'm heart gled to ha'e ye back. There's none like you for makin' kail and none has your hand wi' a scone and a bannock or wi' washing my shirt. As for the bairn—"

And Kirsty, carrying her baby, went into the cottage with her husband.

Prince Ian Direach and His Quest

There was a prince once whose father was king of the western isles. His name was Ian Direach and he was a fine lad, very dear to his parents, loved by all the people. He could ride and swim, shoot with bow and arrows, run and leap better than most young men, and he had, besides a skilled hand on the harp and a sweet voice for singing. Life was very happy in the king's house and throughout the isles until the much-loved queen died, and then there was deep sorrow. The king, the prince and all the people mourned for her, and most of them mourned for a long time in faithful grief; but the king forgot, and within a year he married again.

The new queen was jealous of Ian Direach and he knew that if she could, she would do him harm, lay some spell upon him. Fortunately he had some knowledge of spells and was on his guard. He was always courteous to her and tried to please her.

One day he went out after game. He saw a beautiful blue falcon flying in the air and aimed an arrow carefully, but the flight of the falcon was so swift that the arrow only touched her and one blue feather fell, which Ian Direach picked up and put into his bag. It was growing late, and he went back to his father's house.

His stepmother came to meet him, looking sour-faced.

"What game have you brought for supper?" she asked.

"Only this," Ian told her, taking the blue feather from his bag.

"Then I bind a spell upon you: that you go in search of the falcon from which you shot the feather, and do not return without her."

"And I bind you with a spell," retorted Ian, "that until I return, you stand on the roof of the house facing the wind and the rain."

Both spells were instantly binding. The prince went off, leaving the queen standing on the roof, where his spell had placed her, facing the wind and the rain; whether they blew from east or west, north or south, she was compelled to turn that way. Ian went travelling through wood and plain, by sea and river, coming late one night into a dark wood. Tired, hungry, disheartened, he lay down under a tree and fell asleep. Presently he felt the touch of a soft, warm body, and heard a voice:

"Will you waken, Prince Ian? It is myself, Gil Martin the fox, speaking to you, and wanting to be your friend. I have brought you some supper; it is only the hoof and jaw of a sheep, that's all I could get today, but it's better than nothing."

Ian Direach awoke. Here was Gil Martin the fox with his russet coat and long snout and bright eyes. The pair of them gathered sticks for a fire, roasted the hoof and the jaw and ate their supper in comfort and friendship.

"Now tell me where you are going and what it is you are seeking," said the fox. The prince told him the whole tale of his quest.

"Well, I can tell you where to find the blue falcon. She is in the house of the giant with five heads and five necks and five humps, and that is not far from here. Go you there in the morning and ask for work. You are a fine hand with birds and beasts and the giant will be glad to have you. You will see the blue falcon. Bide your time and there will come a day when the giant will leave you by yourself, in charge of his birds and beasts, and then you may take the falcon. But remember to wrap her in a cloth and not let her see the sun and not let so much as a feather of her touch anything in the house—or else, misfortune will come upon you."

The prince thanked this good comrade and in the morning went off cheerfully, and before long came to the house of the giant with the five heads, five necks and five humps on his back. He roared at Ian:

"What do you want?" And Ian answered boldly:

"I've come seeking work."

"What can you do?"

"Anything you ask. I'll herd and milk your cows, herd your sheep and your pigs, care for your birds."

"Well, that would suit me," said the giant. "I'll give you a chance."

The prince had spoken truly when he said he could look after all the birds and beasts. He was good with all kinds of creatures, they knew this and were good with him. He saw the blue falcon and tended and exercised her every day. The giant watched him closely, and was satisfied.

"I see you can take care of them," he said one day. "So I'll be off on a journey to visit my brother. It is many a year since I've done that for I could not leave my birds and my beasts."

As soon as the giant was out of sight, Ian took the falcon, wrapped her in a cloth and went out of the house. But the sun was bright and its rays pierced the cloth and excited the bird. She gave a spring—the tip of a feather pierced the cloth and touched the doorpost which let out a scream. Instantly the giant came back.

And now, thought Ian, he would be killed. But the giant said only: "So you want my falcon? You may have her if you bring me the Sword of Light which is guarded by the Seven Women of the Farthest Isle."

And that was that. Who the Women were or where was their island Ian did not know. As he walked off he was met by Gil Martin the fox.

"Och, but you're the foolish lad! Didn't I tell you to be careful," said the fox, but he said it kindly. "Now I suppose I must turn myself into a boat and take you to the Isle of the Seven Women."

And as soon as they came down to the edge of the sea he had changed himself into a boat. Ian got in and was carried over the waves, a long way, to the island where the Seven Women lived.

Again Ian offered his services in any way they might desire. He was set to clean the house and all the dishes, the wine flagons, the pots and pans. This he did so well, putting a good shine on everything, that one of the women said to her sisters:

"Sure, we may give him the Sword of Light to polish," and they agreed. They were pleased with his work, he made the sword shine like the sun, and they left him more and more to work by himself. One day when they had all gone to different parts of the island Ian thought it a good moment to take the sword. Gil Martin had promised to be ready to change himself again into a boat and carry him away. Before they had parted he had warned Ian not to let even the tip of the sword touch anything in the house.

Very carefully, the prince took down the sword in its sheath, put it over his shoulder and walked out of the house. But the tip of the sheath touched the door lintel and there was a screech from it that brought the seven women rushing back, all together. Ian feared they would do him violence, but they merely said:

"So you want the Sword of Light? You shall have it—if you bring us the brown colt of the King of Erin."

And how to do that, Ian had no idea at all.

As he walked off, he met Gil Martin who shook his head and reproached him:

"Bungled it again, have you? Well, well, it must be another voyage, to Erin this time."

Again he turned himself into a boat, and carried Ian Direach over the western sea to Erin. Ian landed, and received instructions from Gil Martin, ending with the caution:

"And when you have the brown colt, be sure that neither hoof nor tail touch any part of the stable."

Ian went up to the king's house and offered his services.

"What can you do?" asked the king.

"Anything, but especially anything with horses," answered Ian.

"It happens that I'm in need of a groom," said the king, "so let me see what you can do."

Ian spoke truly when he said he was good with horses. He worked so well that the king, in high approval, said one day:

"You're fit now to take care of my best horse of all, the brown colt."

The colt was a beauty and under Ian's care he became more beautiful than ever, perfectly groomed, his brown coat shining. The king was delighted.

"I'm off hunting tomorrow," he told Ian, "and I'll trust you to look after the colt."

Here was Ian's chance. The king had no sooner ridden out of sight, over the hill, than Ian saddled the colt and led him from the stable, ready to mount and ride away; the king would never catch him for the colt ran swifter than the wind. But as he led the colt out the creature swished his tail, it touched the stable door, and there was a screech that brought the king back riding at top speed.

He looked less angry than Ian feared.

"So it's taking my colt, you would. Well, you may have him—if you bring the daughter of the King of France here, from over the sea, to be my bride.'

And how was he to do that? Ian wondered miserably. He wandered off down to the shore and there he met Gil Martin coming from behind a rock.

"Ach, you're the foolish one. Will you never pay heed to what I tell you? Well, I suppose I must turn myself into a ship again, but maybe this will be the last time. Sit down now and eat the food I've found for you and then we'll be off."

The prince ate gratefully, the fox again became a ship and took Ian aboard.

"Take your harp with you, but leave it in the hold, when we come to France," the fox ordered him.

Ian had not been playing his harp much, of late, but he had it with him, slung over his shoulder.

They sailed over a rough sea to the coast of France, where the fox-ship came to shore in a rocky inlet. Ian had had his instructions and now he landed and walked up towards a castle. The King and Queen of France and their beautiful daughter saw him, and came out to discover who he was and whence he came. The prince had a fine tale ready, of many adventures and near-shipwreck, to which they listened entranced.

"You're welcome here," said the king graciously. "And you'll be ready for your dinner. But first we would like to see the ship that has brought you safely and so far."

"And I'll be glad to show Your Majesties that," answered Ian courteously.

He led the way down to the shore. As they came near the ship they heard sweet music from the harp in the hold, which delighted the princess. The king and queen, having looked at the ship which was somewhat battered, would have returned to the castle, but the princess begged to be taken on board, to listen to the music and to find the harper. The minute she was safe aboard, with Ian's help, the fox-ship moved off swiftly into the sea, away and over to Erin.

"Where are you taking me?" demanded the princess. "You must take me back at once to France."

"Ah, don't bid me do that," said Ian Direach. "Just listen to what I have to tell you."

He told her then the true tale of his wanderings.

"So now it's to Erin I'm taking you, to be married to the king."

"I don't want to be married to him," said the princess. "I'd rather be married to you."

This pleased Prince Ian very much but he did not quite see how it could be managed.

They came swiftly to the shores of Erin and there they landed. The fox-ship turned into Gil Martin again.

"Now listen to me," he said to Prince Ian. "The princess must hide there in that cave and I'll turn myself into a princess as lovely as she is. You'll conduct me to the king who will give you the brown colt. Then ride the colt down to the sea and wait for me."

The princess obediently hid in the cave. The fox became a beautiful princess whom Ian led up towards the king's fine house. The King of Erin was outside and saw them coming. He was full of joy and he had the colt saddled with a gold saddle, bridled with a silver bridle.

"So you've brought my bride," he said to Ian. "Take the brown colt, now, and welcome."

He bowed low to the fox-princess, offered her his hand and led her into his castle.

"There is a crown here, awaiting you, with many jewels," he told her, leading her to a great chest in the hall. As he bent to open it the fox-princess suddenly changed back into Gil Martin, leapt on the king's back and knocked him down. His head struck the chest with such a hard blow that he became unconscious; and Gil Martin the Fox ran off, down to the shore.

There he found Ian Direach with the real princess and the brown colt safely hidden in the cave.

"Come on," said Gil Martin. "I'm changing myself again into a ship to take you to the island of the Seven Women. Once we're there I'll turn myself into a brown colt and you'll take me to them. The princess and the real colt must hide again in a cave."

Swiftly the fox-ship took them over the sea to the island of the Seven Women, and there the princess and the brown colt hid in a cave. Gil Martin became another colt and was led by Ian Direach up to the house of the Seven Women who came rushing out to meet him screaming with joy.

"So you've brought us the brown colt! The Sword of Light is yours now," and one of them brought out the sword and gave it to Ian.

Then the eldest leapt upon the fox-colt, and one by one her sisters followed, sitting on her back or on the back of the colt which seemed to be long enough and strong enough to hold them all. Off they rode at full gallop, laughing and shouting, and off went Prince Ian very quickly, down to the sea-shore, carrying the Sword of Light in its sheath. He had not long to wait before Gil Martin came to him. The fox-colt had carried the women to the top of a high hill, then he had kicked up his hind legs and thrown them all off, down the hill, down, down, down. Then he had changed back into a fox and come to take Ian, the princess and the real colt on their way. Again he became a ship and carried them to land not far from the house of the giant with seven heads and seven necks and seven humps.

"Let the princess and the brown colt stay here," said Gil Martin, "and let her keep the Sword of Light. Now I shall turn myself into another Sword which you must carry to the giant; then be off as fast as you can back to the princess."

Ian Direach obediently carried the fox-sword to the giant who seized it and told Ian:

"So you've found it for me! Well, you'll find the falcon there; put her in a bag and be off."

This Ian very gladly and quickly did. He came back to the princess who was holding the real Sword of Light. Up at the castle the giant was playing with the fox-sword, whirling it round his heads; and in a minute or so he had whirled it through his five necks and cut off his five heads. Gil Martin, taking his true shape again, came back to the princess and Ian Direach who were waiting with the brown colt and the real Sword of Light.

"So now you are near the end of your adventure," he told Ian. "Take the princess up behind you on the colt and hold the sword in front of you. Ride back to your father's house where you'll find your stepmother where you left her, standing on the roof. But keep the Sword in front of your face, the sheath touching your nose, or else she will be turning you into a bundle of sticks and setting light to you. And good luck to you."

"And the thanks of our hearts to you," replied Ian. "Will you not be coming with us."

"Och, maybe I'll be seeing you again," said Gil Martin, "but off with you now."

Off rode Ian Direach, with the princess behind him on the golden saddle of the brown colt with the silver bridle. Ian held the Sword of Light before his face, the sheath touching his nose. When they came to his father's house, he saw his stepmother standing on the roof, as he had compelled her to stand, facing the wind and the rain. She was drenched and bedraggled, she looked furious, and she began to screech at Ian. She would have uttered another spell but before she could say a word he had turned her into a bundle of sticks. Then he set fire to her, and that was the end of her and her wickedness.

The king came running out to welcome his son; he did not shed a tear about his queen whose evil nature he had discovered and hated. The people all over the western isles were full of joy at the return of their prince, and gave him and his bride a great welcome.

There was a fine wedding feast. Word was sent to the King and Queen of France who came swiftly over the sea, very well pleased by this end of the adventure. A grand welcome awaited them, but the guest of honour was Gil Martin the fox.

To him Ian Direach offered any reward he could name, but all Gil Martin wanted was the friendship of the prince and his bride; and this was his already. Ian Direach then had the idea of ordering that the good fox was henceforth to be allowed to take any food he wanted, lamb or goose, duck or bird. So that was the happy ending of the quest.

12

The Two Herdsmen

The Laird of Lochbuie in Mull had two herdsmen, Hector and Ian. Hector's wife Ishbel went to visit Ian's wife Morag, and found her stirring a pot over the fire, a pot which gave out no savoury smell as good broth or stew would do.

"What are you cooking there?" she asked, being an inquisitive woman, although good-natured enough.

"It is just some oatmeal brochan for my man's dinner," Morag told her. Brochan means broth but oatmeal and water with nothing else in it hardly deserves the name.

"And is that all you have to give the poor man?" said Ishbel. "All the years we have served Lochbuie we have never lacked a bit of meat for the pot, and vegetables too. Wait you, and I'll send Hector over, and he and Ian can be going out tonight and killing one of the laird's cattle. He'll never miss it, with the herds he has."

"Och, I'd be afraid to let Ian do that," Morag replied. "Lochbuie is a great chief, he has the power to hang a man for that, or less than that."

"But he's a kind man too, and besides he need never know," said Ishbel, and off she went.

She usually had her own way and that night, after dark, Hector arrived at Ian's door. Morag had told Ian what Ishbel had said, and he was ready for the adventure, especially after the poor supper he had had. Meanwhile Morag had thought of a plan. She sent Ian out of the house first, and spoke softly to Hector.

"When you've killed the ox, bring it here to me. Tell Ian to stay back. Then if any questions are asked I can say that my man did not take it, and Ishbel can say you did not bring any ox to your house. There will be no lies told, and we shall all be safe."

"That is a good plan and you are the clever one," agreed Hector.

The two men went off. They had to go through a wood to reach the field where the cattle were. Now Morag had been right to feel afraid. Only that morning Lochbuie had caught a cattle thief, not one of his own servants, and had hanged him from a tall tree. Neither Ian nor Hector had heard about it. They stopped by that very gallows tree to light a fire. Ian would keep watch while Hector went to take the ox.

Meanwhile, up at the castle, the chief and his guests had dined well and were drinking merrily. They talked about the hanged man (a hanging did not greatly distress anyone in those days except no doubt the family of the victim). The guests made a wager with their host that he had no one in the castle brave enough to go to the wood and take the brogues or shoes off the hanged man and bring them back.

Lochbuie accepted the wager. He sent for one of his servants, a man named MacFadyen, and asked if he would do this feat.

"Indeed and I will," said MacFadyen who did not lack courage.

Off he went, but when he came near the gallows tree he saw a fire and a man sitting beside it. This was too much for him. He went back in fear to the castle and told the chief:

"I have not brought you the brogues, for the corpse himself had come down from the tree and lit a fire and was sitting there warming himself."

Lochbuie's guests laughed. "Do you think we'll believe that? It's only a tale to excuse your own cowardice," they said.

MacFadyen did not like that at all. Then another servant, a lame man called Dougal, spoke:

"If I had two good feet I would go and bring back the brogues and let the chief win his wager."

"Would you now?" said MacFadyen. "Then you can have two good legs and two good feet under you, for I'll carry you there myself."

He took Dougal up on his back and carried him to the gallows tree. When he saw the man sitting by the fire, the lame man was terrified.

"I'm not liking this at all. Let us be going home," he said.

"We will not!" MacFadyen told him. "It was yourself who wanted to come."

At that moment Ian looked up, saw the dim shape of a man with something on his back, thought it was Hector with the ox, and asked:

"Are you there?"

"I am here," answered MacFadyen.

"Have you got it?"

"I have."

"Is it fat or lean?" asked Ian, and MacFadyen in terror replied:

"Fat or lean, here it is," set down the lame man and ran for home. Dougal came hobbling and limping after him as fast as he could, faster than anyone would have thought possible for a lame man.

"They must be two of the laird's men sent to spy on us," said Ian to himself. "I'd better not wait here. I'll away up to the castle and make my peace with the laird."

He ran off, after Dougal who thought he was being followed by the hanged man and was more terrified than ever. One by one the three came to the castle, MacFadyen well ahead. He rushed in, and when they asked him:

"Well, have you brought us the brogues this time?" he gasped:

"I have not and I will not be going back there. The hanged man was down from the gallows, sitting by a fire, and he asked me had I got it, and was it fat or lean, the one that I was carrying. By this time he will have eaten up poor Dougal."

At that moment came a loud knock at the door, and the voice of Dougal crying:

"Let me in, let me in. Yon one from the gallows is after me."

They let him in and he told how he had run from the place.

Then came another knock, and another voice crying:

"Let me in! Bring me to Lochbuie, bring me to himself."

But no one would open the door—they thought it was the hanged man.

The voice called again:

"Lochbuie, let me in. I am your herdsman, Ian."

They knew the voice then, and they opened the door. Ian came in and very humbly and timidly told the laird everything: how Hector and he, in their hunger, had gone to steal an ox, Hector to take it, himself to wait by the fire. He had thought he saw Hector come back with the ox on his back, and so had asked:

"Have you got it? Is it fat or lean?"

It was such a good tale and so well told that Lochbuie and his guests roared with laughter, and the laird had no notion at all of punishing Ian. Indeed he may have felt a bit penitent for having thoughtlessly kept his people so poor. They gave Ian plenty to eat and drink, and kept him there until dawn, making him tell the story again and again.

They admitted that Dougal and MacFadyen had some cause to be frightened, seeing what they took for a corpse sitting there by the fire.

Meanwhile Hector had done his part. Having killed a good fat ox, he heaved it up on his back and went to the fire in the wood to show Ian. But no one was there.

"Och, where are you?" he cried and began to look around him. He had not far to look for there in the shadows he saw the man hanging on the gallows tree.

"Ochone, they have taken Ian and hanged him," he lamented. "And now they will take and hang me. It is all the fault of these women, sending us out."

Sorrowfully he laid down the ox, cut down the dead man from the tree and took him on his back. He had no thought or desire for that fat ox. Sadly and wearily he went stumbling through the wood to Ian's house and knocked at the door. Morag who had been waiting and listening, opened it at once.

"Have you brought it? Where is Ian?"

"It is no ox I have brought but your own man Ian. While I was after the ox they came and took him and hanged him from the gallows tree. Now do not be roaring and crying like that."

The poor woman had begun to weep and who could blame her? She was blaming herself for sending Ian out on that business.

"We are in danger, for the laird will be after us. Let us bury poor Ian in the yard and say no more about it; and I'll be off home," said Hector.

He dug a hole and they buried the corpse of the man from the gallows tree. Then Hector went home.

Not long after, while poor Morag was sitting alone, weeping, Ian came back in fine fettle, full of the laird's good meat and drink. He knocked on the door. There was no sound from within the house. He knocked again and called:

"Let me in, Morag. It's myself come safe home."

"It is not," replied Morag. "You have been hanged and buried."

"I have not been hanged yet. It's myself alive and well, though where Hector is and what he has done with the ox I cannot tell."

"It is not yourself and you shall not come in." Morag had stopped weeping. She thought it was Ian's ghost come to haunt her. The door stayed shut.

The best thing to do now, thought Ian, was to go to Hector and Ishbel. There he knocked at their door, calling:

"Let me in. It's myself, Ian."

"It is not," replied Hector. "You have been hanged and buried."

"Come you to the window. Look out and see if I have been hanged," Ian told him, and Hector obeyed.

"Och man, I see now that it is yourself and you have not been hanged at all. Isn't that the wonder of the world! Come you in now, and tell us how you escaped."

Ian came in and was given a dram. They sat by the fire, he and Ishbel and Hector, talking and going over the whole business. Ian could explain about the poor hanged man, Hector about dropping the ox and taking the corpse on his back.

"I'd better be going back to Morag," said Ian. "And you'd better be coming with me to tell her it's myself."

They went, the three of them and this time Morag opened the door and was heart-thankful to see her man alive and well. They told her the whole story.

"And now we'd better go up to the castle and tell the rest of it to Lochbuie," said Ian, and off the two herdsmen went. The end of the tale amused the laird and his guests—and Lochbuie paid the wager, for none of his servants had, after all, brought back the brogues of the hanged man. He did not grudge that and he did not grudge the ox to Ian and Hector. The story was worth it. He sent them each a good bag of meal besides. So if it was meal-brochan or broth Morag made that day she had a good bit of meat to put into it.

13

King Orfeo and his Queen

King Orfeo reigned in a northern isle, with his Queen, Eurydis. They loved each other dearly and were loved by their people, for they were all that a king and queen should be. Eurydis was lovely and gentle, kind and gay, Orfeo was tall and strong, gallant and brave. He was both wise and benevolent, ruling his people well, caring as much for the common folk as for the great lords and nobles. And to all these virtues he added the gift of music; he was the finest harper in the land.

Orfeo and Eurydis had charming children. There seemed nothing left for them to desire. They lived in joy and in kindness.

One day the king and his lords and huntsmen rode to the hunt. The queen, with her ladies and the children saw them go, with horn blowing. Then Eurydis sat with her ladies on a green lawn, embroidering a fine tunic for the king. The children were playing with their nurse. Orfeo thought of them as he rode out and thought of them again as he rode back from the hunt. They would come to meet him with a loving welcome and he and his lords would tell the queen, her ladies and the children about the hunt. There would be a bath and fine clothes laid out to wear, one of the queen's embroidered tunics; then a feast for which they were already very hungry, with wine and music, the king himself gladly granting the wish of the company for a tune from his harp: a song, then a dancing tune to set them all dancing in the hall.

But as they came to the palace gates all those bright dreams fled from the king and his company; for they were met by weeping women and by children sobbing their hearts out. Eurydis the queen was nowhere among them.

"Where is the queen? Where is my Eurydis? What has happened?" asked the king.

"My lord, it is great sorrow." The king's steward who was old and wise and gentle answered with sorrowful compassion. "The King of Faery came and touched our Queen with his rod, an ice-cold dart which froze her as if in a swoon. Then he took her cold hand and led her out of the garden, out from the gates into the wood and beyond, none can say where, for none could follow. We were spell-bound."

The king listened as if himself spell-bound by grief. But he could and did move and act. He dismounted from his horse, he sent for his harp and he set forth alone, forbidding anyone to follow him, out of the gate, into the wood and beyond, no man could tell where, and he himself could not say whether the way were long or short, until he came to a great, grey stone which seemed to block the entrance into a bleak hillside.

Orfeo took his harp and played. He played a sad tune from his own sad heart and it would have broken your heart to hear it. Then he played a happy tune, lilting and gay, which would have lifted up the saddest heart to hear it. Finally he played a dancing tune, a daft tune such as he had often played in his palace to set all the lords and ladies, the servants, the children, dancing madly together and laughing for joy. When he had ended that, the great stone swung back opening a deep hall, and a voice called:

"Come in, King Orfeo, and play to us."

Orfeo entered the hall of the King of Faery, a place of shadows and strange, glimmering lights. The King of Faery sat on his throne and beside him sat Eurydis, pale, still, frozen, as in a swoon or a dream.

"Play to us, Orfeo," bade the king, and Orfeo played. He played from his own sad heart a tune of sorrow and of loss and longing, a tune to pierce the hearts of all who heard it; the shadow of death was in it. The faery folk listened as to something strange, beyond their knowledge; for some hold that they know nothing of death or of the pain it brings. Then Orfeo played a happy tune, lilting and gay, full of light and laughter, of the song of birds, the ripple of water, bringing the thought of flowers, of young love, of old and faithful love, of such happiness as those faery folk had not heard before, and they all laughed for joy. Finally Orfeo played a dancing tune, a daft tune, a tune which compelled them all to dance as even they, the dancing people, had never danced before. Only their king sat still, his eyes upon the harper; and Eurydis sat still, as if frozen or spell-bound.

The tune ended, the dancers sank happily exhausted on the floor, on seats and cushions. Their king then spoke, gently and courteously:

"Thank you, King Orfeo. You have played for our delight, played such music as we have never heard before. Now, what do you desire as reward? Ask what you will and you shall have it."

King Orfeo bowed and answered:

"I ask for my queen, Eurydis."

"She is yours," replied the King of Faery. He rose, and turned to the still white figure by his side. He touched her with his rod. She stirred a little, rose and smiled at Orfeo, her face flushed with colour, her eyes glowed with love.

She walked a few steps towards him and he came to take her hand. They turned to the King of Faery, Eurydis curtsied deeply, Orfeo bowed.

"We thank you, King."

Then they walked down the hall together, Orfeo with his harp slung over his shoulder; down to the doorway, out and away. The great grey stone swung and closed behind them. They walked in light.

Whether the way were long or short they could not tell but the road was sure and smooth. As they came near the palace they saw a crowd of waiting, sorrowful people, their children in front, gently held by nurse and kind ladies. Then there was a cry of joy. The children came running, were gathered up and held in the arms of mother and father; they were surrounded by a joyful crowd, calling blessings on their king and queen, thanksgiving for their return.

Orfeo and Eurydis led them back to the palace. That night there was a feast even more splendid and more joyful than that which had followed their wedding and the christening of their babies. At the end of the feasting, Orfeo took his harp and played a most joyful tune, yet with a little wistful air of enchantment in it; the wistfulness vanished as morning mist will drift away; the music was pure joy, a dancing tune such as even he had never played before.

14

Tam Lin

At Carterhaugh on the Borders, where many a queer thing has happened and there is many a door to Elfland, and it is better not to go in, there was a fairy well; and this was the rhyme about it:

> "Oh, I forbid you, maidens a',
> Wha wear gowd on your hair,
> To come or gae by Carterhaugh,
> For young Tam Lin is there."

Tam Lin was a lad who had been taken away to Elfland and had an uncanny fame; the girl who lingered by that well would come under his power and must pay a fee; this might be a ring or a silken cloak or her maidenhood.

There was a lass called Janet, or the Lady Janet, for she was daughter to a great lord. She wore gold on her hair, and her hair was golden, a gold ring, a silk gown and a mantle as green as grass which became her well, golden-fair as she was with the colours of spring. Her father was wise as well as kind, and he knew his daughter, a bonny lass, proud and wilful, but brave and loyal too—a girl of spirit, more likely to be allured than frightened by the warning about the well.

So one day she went off by herself to Carterhaugh, not riding but walking swiftly, her green skirts kilted above her knees, her yellow hair wound in a plait round her head. When she came to the well she saw no man, but a horse was grazing there—and it was Tam Lin's horse. A rose-bush grew by the well, and Janet pulled a spray of two intertwining roses. Hardly had she done so, before she could fasten it to her gown with a golden pin than young Tam Lin appeared, pretending to be stern, but laughing:

"Janet, Janet, my bold bonny lass, why do you come to my well without leave from me, and pull my roses?"

"Carterhaugh is on my father's land," Janet told him proudly, but her eyes were warm and sparkling. "And I'll come here with or without your leave, and pull a rose if I will."

"So?" said Tam Lin, taking her by the hand. "Then you must pay my fee."

He put his arm round her and led her away, without any word or motion of refusal or resistance from her. At the end of that golden day she went back to her father's castle, still with her green mantle, still with her gold ring, but without her maidenhood.

Janet went again to the well, her green gown kilted above her knees, her hair plaited round her head; she went swiftly, walking and running, and at the well she found Tam Lin's horse, as before. She pulled a double rose, two roses on one stem, and Tam himself appeared.

"Tell me," said Janet, "for His Sake Who died on the tree, were you ever in holy chapel with Christian folk, are you a christened man?"

"Aye, indeed I am. My grandfather is the Earl of Roxburghe; he took me to live with him, and one day a sore evil befell me. It was a bitter cold day, with a snell wind blowing; we were riding home from the hunt, I fell from my horse by some enchantment, and the Queen of Fairies took me captive, and kept me in her green hill. There I have been compelled to bide for nearly seven years. It is a pleasant place, fair Elfland, but oh Janet, I must tell you a woeful thing. Every seven years the queen must pay tribute to hell, and often it is a mortal man she gives; and I fear this time it will be myself, for the seven years are up. Yet there is hope, Janet. Tonight is Hallowe'en and tomorrow is All Hallows. Tonight, if you will, you may save me, Janet."

"Tell me, my love, how I may," said Janet, looking at him with steadfast eyes.

"At the mirk hour of midnight the fairy host will ride this way, and I shall be among them."

"Tell me, my love, how I shall know you in the mirk night, in so strange a company?"

"Let the rider on the black horse pass, Janet, and the rider on the brown; but when one on a milk-white steed comes riding by, then run, Janet, seize the horse by the bridle and pull his rider down; for that rider will be I myself. My right hand will be gloved, my left hand bare; my bonnet will be cocked, my hair combed down beneath it. So you will know me, Janet; hold me in your arms and save me.

"Hold me fast, for the queen will put spells upon me. I shall turn first to a lizard, then to an adder; to a bear, and to a fierce lion. But still hold me fast, Janet, loathsome as I may seem. I shall be turned to a bar of red-hot iron, and to burning lead. Throw me then into the water of the well and I shall become myself again, a mortal man, naked as a newborn child. Wrap me in your mantle, Janet, cover me well—and I shall be saved."

Janet listened and promised. That night she went back to the well in the deep, deep mirk of Hallowe'en. There was neither moonlight nor starlight, neither sound nor sight of humankind. At midnight Janet heard the bridles ring, and she was glad of that as of any earthly thing, for it meant that the fairy host was near, her own true love riding with it.

There was a glimmer of light now, and she saw a rider on a black horse, and let him ride on; then came one on a brown horse but he too rode by without word or motion from Janet. She waited, wrapped in her green cloak. At last came the rider on the milk-white horse glimmering in the dark. Janet ran forward, seized the bridle, and pulled the rider to the ground, holding him fast in her arms. At once she felt herself holding a lizard, then the lizard became a loathsome adder. But Janet held firm. The soft, wriggling shape became a great rough bear of a strength that nearly overcame her, but still she held; then a lion of terrible fierceness and Janet's heart nearly failed her for fear; but still she held fast. The shape became a bar of red-hot iron that seemed to burn her to the bone, then a piece of burning lead—that, she threw into the deep water of the well.

From the dark, cool depths rose a naked man; her own love Tam. Mindful of his bidding she threw off her own green cloak, wrapping it round him. There he stood, looking at her, his grey eyes full of love and joy and thankfulness for her leal courage.

As they stood close together an angry voice shrieked from a bush of broom. The Fairy Queen was mad with rage; but she could do nothing, for a magic more powerful than hers had rescued Tam Lin.

"A curse on you," she cried to Janet. "You have stolen away my best knight. As for you, Tam Lin, had I known what I know now, I would have plucked out your bonny grey eyes and given you eyes of wood!"

But her rage meant nothing to the happy lovers, who fled away, swiftly and safely, to Janet's father's castle. There they were welcomed joyfully, and there they were married. And they lived together in great bliss all their lives long; and the bairn that was born to them was the bonniest in all the countryside.

15

The King of Albainn and The Big Lad

This is a story about a young King of Albainn and his sister the princess. They were devoted to each other and to the old king, their father, and when, one dreadful day, a great giant came and carried off the princess, there was such grief that the old king died of it. The young king looked like dying too, for he could do nothing but sit by his father's grave, lamenting. The people were sorely anxious about him, but no one could help him. Then one day a big ugly lad came to him, and said:

"There is a bond laid upon me to become your servant for a year and a day."

"I do not want you," replied the young king. "You would frighten all the others"—which was rude, but the lad was truly fearsome to look at.

"I can't help that," said the lad good-naturedly, "and you can't help taking me as your servant, for we are bound together. Another thing too: you must give over this foolish grieving. It does no good to your father, and it will bring harm to you and to your kingdom. I'll come to you tomorrow."

The king went home. Next morning a fine-looking lad was brought to him, who asked:

"Are you in want of a servant, King of Albainn?"

"I am not," said the young king, "for yesterday I had one wished on me, and an ugly fellow he was. Were it not for that, I'd gladly take you."

The lad turned himself round, and showed the king the cheerful, ugly face he had worn yesterday.

"Is this your ugly servant?" he asked.

"It is," replied the king. "And I'll be glad to have you; but if it's all the same to yourself, I'd rather have you handsome."

"Fine," agreed the lad, turning himself round again, and showing his handsome face. "You will remember I bade you give over your grieving," he said.

But the king thought he would go just once more to his father's grave. There he fell asleep, and in his sleep heard a voice bidding him waken, then asking him:

"What is it that has made the King of Erin go sad and cheerless, these seven years?"

"That I cannot tell," said the King of Albainn.

"If you cannot find out, I will have your head," threatened the voice.

The young king went home, looking sadder than ever.

"What ails you?" asked the big lad.

The king told him about the voice that had asked him what kept the King of Erin sad and cheerless these seven years.

"Well, that is a question many a hero has been asked and has tried to answer; and none of those who went to find out has ever returned.

Did I not tell you to give over your grieving at the grave of your father? Now we must be going, you and I, to try to find the answer to this question. If I cannot help you, at least I will not be hindering you."

Next day they set off, and towards nightfall the king asked:

"Where shall we be tonight?"

"With your sister and the giant," the lad told him.

Soon afterwards, they came to the cave where the giant held the princess captive. The giant was not there himself, which was a good thing. The princess was in great joy at seeing her brother again, but at the same time in great fear that the giant might return and kill him.

"Where is he?" asked the big lad.

"Out on the hill, hunting game," the princess told him.

"I'll go and meet him there," said the lad. "And let you two wait here and make our supper."

Off went the big lad, and before long he saw the giant who shouted to him:

"Come over here to me and sing me a song."

For wicked as he was, this giant liked music. The lad went over behind him, singing a song to lull him: then with his sword he killed the giant, cutting off his big ugly head; and no one need grieve for him because he was a bad giant. The lad took the head back to the cave.

"There's the giant's head for you," he said to the princess cheerfully. "Maybe we'd better bury it."

"I knew you were a hero," said the princess, crying a little for relief. "And now, tell me where you and my brother are going."

There had been no time for the King of Albainn to tell her anything. So the lad told her all about their journey, and the question the king must answer.

"I've heard about that question," she said, "and I've seen many a hero set out to find the answer. But never a one came back."

They had supper then, with a good deal of loving talk between brother and sister, and more cheerfulness on both of them than had been for a long time. The princess showed the king and the lad their sleeping-place, and they all slept well; when they rose in the morning the princess had breakfast ready for them. Now there was in the cave a beautiful white bird that could sing any bird song ever heard from bush or tree.

"If we could take that bird with us," said the lad, "its song would get us an audience with the King of Erin."

"You may have it," said the princess, "if you will promise to take care of it."

"Indeed we will; and if we come back safely the bird will be with us."

"And when will you come?"

"If we are alive we will be here again with you in a year."

Then off the lad and the king went, travelling until they reached the palace of the King of Erin. They came to the wall and gate of the palace at nightfall and waited there. As the darkness passed, they saw, in the glimmer of dawn, a row of twelve spikes on the wall. On ten of them was impaled a head.

"So these are the champions who did not come back," said the lad. "Maybe the two spikes that are left are for our heads."

"I am certain of that," agreed the King of Albainn. "But we cannot draw back."

"Och well, it may not happen like that after all," said the lad more cheerfully. "Look, now, I am putting the white bird to perch on one of the spikes."

Then to the bird he said: "Sing, now, as you have never sung before."

The bird began to sing. As the notes of its song, sweet, clear and thrilling beyond any birdsong heard before, reached the ears of the King of Erin he looked out; he saw the white bird singing with all its happy heart, and he saw the two wayfarers at the gate.

"Go and bring these two men in and their bird with them," he ordered his servant. "But let none see them enter."

The servant went out, spoke to the young king and the lad, telling them to come in with their bird but let none see them enter. They followed him, carrying the bird. Inside the door of the palace stood the door-keeper. The lad caught him and knocked him on the head; the servant went and told the King of Erin.

"Bring them in, all the same," commanded the King of Erin. "I must hear that bird sing again."

When the servant took that message, the big lad said: "Sure, he may listen to the bird if he will pay for his pleasure."

When they came into the King of Erin's room he asked them:

"And who are you, rough and brutal fellows, knocking my door-keeper on the head like that?"

"I'd never have done it," replied the lad, "if you had not told your servant here that none but himself was to see us come in."

"Well, we'll say no more about it," agreed the King of Erin. "Now let me hear your bird."

The lad set the bird up on top of a cupboard where it began to sing more sweetly than ever. The King of Erin listened, entranced, and when the song was ended he asked:

"And now, what payment do you demand?"

"Only this," replied the lad, "that you tell us what has kept you so sad and cheerless these seven years."

"Would I tell you that when I have told it to none of the brave heroes who have come here in these seven years, and whose heads are now set on the wall? There are two spikes left, and by noon today your two heads will be on them."

"Maybe they will, and maybe they will not," said the lad. "It would be better for you to tell us now, for tell us you will after I've forced you."

But the King of Erin would not tell; so the big lad caught him up and threw him over the cross-beams of the roof one way, and back the other way. This was not at all comfortable, and the King of Erin cried:

"Spare my life and I'll tell you what you want to know."

"That is sensible of you," said the lad.

"Well, then," said the King of Erin, "seven years ago I had company to stay with me and we went hunting. We coursed a hare that led us to a hillside with many caves, and it ran into one of them. We went in after it and found there a giant with his twelve sons.

"'Sit you down, King of Erin, you and your company,' he invited us, and it was not an invitation we were glad to hear. But we sat down together on one side facing him.

"'Will you play the game of the poisoned apple or the game of the hot gridiron?' he asked us, and we chose the game of the apple.

"The giant then threw the apple he was holding at one of my comrades, and the poor man fell dead. I threw it back at him, but he caught it on the point of a knife he held; he threw it again and again, killing a man every time, and catching it on his knife when I threw it back. When all my comrades were dead he took me and roasted me over the fire until I was near dead myself, then threw me out of the cave to crawl home. Is it any wonder that I have been sad and cheerless these seven years, and have told the reason to none?"

"No wonder at all," said the lad kindly. "If we had been with you that day it might have been a different kind of game. But now let us be off to hunt the hare."

"No indeed, I will not go; I will not go through that again," said the King of Erin.

"Oh, won't you?" said the lad. "Maybe you will, after I've thrown you downstairs like a ball."

"Spare me that, and I'll go with you, good lad," said the King of Erin.

The three of them went off together, the two kings and the big lad. Almost at once they met a hare.

"Is that the one?" asked the lad.

"It looks like it," said the King of Erin.

They chased it and were led to the cave; going in, they found the giant sitting with his twelve sons.

"So you have come again to see me," he said to the king, "and with new comrades. Sit you down."

Before he could put the question to them, the big lad put it to him— would he play the game of the hot gridiron or of the poisoned apple? The giant chose the game of the apple, and he threw the apple at the lad. But that one was ready for it, and caught it on the point of his knife, and came to no harm; he threw it back, not at the giant who was also ready for it, but at one of his sons standing behind him; and the young giant fell dead. Again the old giant threw the apple, again the lad caught it and threw it back, killing another son; and so it went on until the twelve sons were killed and the old giant too stupid and amazed to do anything about it.

When the first was killed, the King of Erin laughed, the first laugh out of him for seven years. He laughed again as each young giant fell. Then he and the young King of Albainn helped the lad to seize the old giant, tie him up and roast him over the fire. When that was done he was thrown out of the cave and that was the end of him, and there is no need to be sorry for him or his sons, for they were as bad a lot as could be found anywhere.

The three comrades found much treasure in the cave, taken from many a poor victim. They returned to the King of Erin's palace to feast together; there was no sadness about the king now, but a great cheerfulness and thankfulness. The young King of Albainn and the lad spent another day and a night there, and when they were leaving the King of Erin begged the big lad to stay with him; but he would not; he would go with his own master the young King of Albainn. The King of Erin would have given them any reward they asked, but they wanted nothing, only to be on their way home.

This time they travelled gaily and swiftly, and came to the cave where the princess was awaiting them. Her joy at seeing them was this time without any flaw of fear; great was her joy too at having the white bird again. They had supper together and she heard all their adventure and gave the lad high praise and thanks for all he had done.

They slept well that night, and in the morning set out for their own kingdom, taking the lovely white bird with them, and it was singing for joy. Without adventure and without delay they reached their own palace. The people had been sad and anxious about their young king and grieved about their princess; so now it was the welcome of welcomes they gave them, and the fullness of thanks to the big lad, their champion. There was a feast, finer even than that given by the King of Erin, and a fine telling of tales.

Next day the big lad said:

"I must be leaving you now, King of Albainn. I have done the service it was laid upon me to do."

The young king and his sister would have kept him with them, but he would not stay. They would have given him any reward he asked, but he wanted none.

"This only I ask of you," he said to the young King of Albainn, "that you give over lamenting for your father, and begin to rule your kingdom well, as he ruled it in his life."

16

The Witch of Fife

There was an old man in Fife whose wife was a witch, and whether her magic was black or white or grey the story does not tell. It was probably no worse than grey, and she was a good enough wife to him; but he was inquisitive, and kept asking her where she went at night when she ought to have been at home in bed.

"Sit doun, then, and listen," she said, "and I'll tell you what will make your hair stand stiff on your head, and the sweat drop into your eyes. But ne'er a word out of you about it, or you will suffer a sore pain. On the night of the new moon we met, my cronies and I, in the kirkyard, and we saddled our horses."

"And where got ye horses?" asked the old man, for they were poor folk, they and their neighbours.

"Easy enough," said his wife. "They are witch-horses that never came out of a stable, but from the woods and the hillside. Some are made of the broom and some of the bay tree, and others of hemlock; mine was that, and a fine strong horse he was. They were saddled with fern that was sown by moonlight; and off we rode. Oh, but it was grand, hunting the fox on the hill and the owl in the woods; the fox could not escape us, the owl could not fly fast enough."

"But what good did that do ye, you silly woman? Better have been at home in your bed."

"Listen, and I'll tell you more. We flew on to Ben Lomond, and there we drank right good ale that never was brewed by human hands in any man's barrel; the like of it you've never tasted. Then up arose a wee, wee man from under a great stone on the hillside, and he played his reed-pipe so sweetly that it stilled the wind to listen to it. The curlew and the blackcock flew out of the wood, the white seamew came from Loch Leven, the crow came flying low, peering down to see who was playing that magical tune, the eagle swooped about the mountain listening, listening; the weasels came out of their holes to dance on the hillside in the faint light of midnight, the trout leapt out of the loch to dance; and we danced too, my cronies and I until dawn came up over the sea. Then we rode home, and it is no wonder I was sore wearied next day."

"And what good did it do you, you daft wife? Better at home in your bed."

"The next night of the new moon we went farther: over the sea in a cockle-shell boat with seaweed for sails. The wind blew high, the thunder rolled, the lightning flashed, but we sailed through the green waves, down into the deep, up into the sky on the green hills of water. We slid down into the depths, we were swift as the gale, we shot down like a falling star, we rose and flew through the flying foam. So we came to Norway over the foam and landed there; we took horse, our horses swifter than the fleet greyhound or the deer on the hill, fleeing from the hounds, swifter than the wind. None could flee over the mountain-tops as we did on our swift horses, over snows untrodden by foot, the snows of eternity, on beyond Norway to Lapland where all the fairy folk of the north were holding festival. The witches and wizards, the fairies of the hills, the elves and fauns of the wood, the phantom hunters told of in stories, they were all there, feasting and dancing, and they gave us welcome as very sisters. They washed us in witch-water distilled from the moorland dew, and we blossomed in beauty like the rose that blooms in the Lapland forest."

"Now that," said her husband rudely, "is a lie, the biggest lie you have told; for the worst-looking woman in Fife is comely compared with you."

His witch-wife took no notice of that; she had more to tell:

"Och then the mermaids rose out of the sea, singing so sweetly, you never heard the like. They hung a harp on every cliff, a lyre on every tree; the woods and the sea rang with their music, sweet beyond telling. We drank their wine, sweet and strong it was, too, and slept in the arms of the warlocks. Then from the master of us all we learned the word of power, the word that will bear us through the air wherever we would go, that will unlock every door, break every barrier.

"And last night we met in Maistry's cottage round the hearth. At midnight, by moonlight we spoke the word, we flew up the chimney out and over the fields and the hills, over the Border and down to merry Carlisle; into the Bishop's palace and down to his cellar. Oh, but he keeps good wine. Locks and bars could not hold us out, there was none that saw or heard us, and we drank our fill."

"If that be true," said the old man greedily, "I'll come with you next time you ride. I'll come with you and drink the good red wine."

"You silly old man, little do you know. We were in deadly peril. We stayed too late, when we left it was cock-crow and the grouse was flying, and crying its bickering cry as we flew over the Borders, up by Ettrick. It was cold in the morning dew. As we flew over the Braid

Hills the sun was rising and we saw the king ride out with his lords. They shot at the deer, but some of their arrows pierced us, although they did not see us, and the dew that fell was red with our blood. Oh, it was in sore danger of our lives we were, and glad to come safely home, and it is little wonder I am so weary. Little do you know, you silly old man, or you would not ask to come with us."

"Now, tell me the word. I would not ride your hellish horses or sail through the sea in storm and darkness; but I could flee through the air with the best of you, and drink you all blind."

"No, never, never will I tell you that word. It is a secret among us. It is a word of power that would turn the world upside down and make it worse than hell."

The witch-wife said no more, and her husband said no more; but he was as cunning as he was greedy, and once he had an idea in his head it would not come out. Night after night he kept watch on his wife; and on the next night of the new moon he went stealthily to the cottage and hid there, in a cupboard. He saw his wife and her cronies, all of whom he knew well, enter, and gather round the hearth. At midnight they spoke the word of power and he heard it clearly. Then up the chimney they flew, the old man after them, for he came out from hiding and spoke the word, and found he could fly as well as they. He kept well behind them, the moonlight was fitful and they did not see him. They flew over fields and hills, over the rivers and over the Borders, down to merry Carlisle, into the Bishop's palace and down to his cellar. And there the old man followed them. They drank the Bishop's good wine and danced and were merry, the old man merriest of all and drinking as much as all of them put together. They were women of sense, they had taken warning, they knew when to stop and when to depart. But when they spoke the word of power again, and rose up, flying out of the palace, out of merry Carlisle, away north

over the Border, before the cock crew, the silly old man was lying
behind a barrel, dead drunk, dead asleep. And there he lay until the
Bishop's servants found him.

"And who are you and how came you here?" they demanded,
seizing him roughly and binding him fast. "Every door was bolted
and barred so that no mortal man could enter unaided."

"I'm from Fife," the silly old man told them. "I flew down on the
night wind."

That was the worst thing he could say, for it made him a warlock.
He was dragged off to be tortured and put to death for black magic.
They pricked him and pierced him, they bound his limbs so fast that
the blood came—though some said it was red wine that flowed from
him. Then they dragged him to the market-place where they tied him
to a stake and began to pile wood around his feet, to burn him as a
warlock. The wood was piled as high as his knees, the flames were
catching, the smoke blew up in his face.

He was stupefied by fear and pain; he could not think of the word
of power. He could only lament his own greed and folly, and look
north towards the Border and Scotland and Fife, the road he would
never tread again. The crowd, watching him, then saw an uncanny
sight, which made them turn their eyes from him: something like a
great, black bird, flying high above the city, above the market-place.
It came swooping down, down to the old man bound to the stake.

Then he saw that it was his own witch-wife who had remembered
him and come to save him. Was he not glad to see her? She put a red
cap on his head and whispered a word—the word of power—in his
ear. He spoke it; his chains fell off, the flames sank down, he rose
high above the stake, above the heads of the people, higher and higher,
and away he flew following the great, black bird-like shape that was
his wife.

They flew over the Eden river, over the Border hills. His arms were widespread like wings, his feet stuck out behind, his coat-tails flapped in the wind. Before he vanished from sight of the city he looked down at it and laughed. His laugh came back to the crowd like the cry of a wild goose. Then he vanished, and that was the last sound and sight they had of him, the last time he spoke the word of power or flew after his wife and her cronies.

No wine was worth such a price. Thereafter he pestered his wife no more with questions or demands, but let her go her own way, while he stayed cannily at home in Fife.

17

Kilmeny

Kilmeny was the loveliest girl in all the Border country, yet she had not a throng of wooers like other girls less beautiful. Her beauty had something withdrawn about it; there was no coldness in it, nothing elfin, only an air about her as about a nun. She was gentle and courteous, loving and gracious.

So when one day Kilmeny went up the glen and did not return at dusk, there was no malicious gossip, never a jest about her having gone to meet a lad or run off with a sweetheart. She did not come back that night or next morning. Day after day passed without news of her. People came down from the hill farms, they came from the far glens, they gathered at sheep-shearing, at harvest, at fair and market, but none had a word of having seen Kilmeny.

Her mother and father grieved for her as dead. Had she fallen into a deep pool in the river, or into the loch? Mass was said for her, many tears were shed, and dried. Life must go on.

Then, late, late one evening in the gloaming, Kilmeny came home.

It was the hour of stillness and rest, when folk are gathered round the fireside, the bairns are in bed. She came as quietly as she had departed, came gently back to her family. She was unharmed, she was lovelier than ever.

> "Kilmeny, Kilmeny, where have you been?
>   Where gat ye that joup o' the lily sheen,
> That bonny snood o' the birk so green?
>   Kilmeny, Kilmeny, where have ye been?"

Kilmeny was dressed neither in plain country garments nor in silk or velvet such as a fine lady might wear, but in textures and colours as delicate as flowers, and as flowers more rare than any that grew in that glen.

> "Kilmeny looked up wi' a lovely grace;
>   But no smile was seen on Kilmeny's face."

—though the face was sweeter and gentler even than before, with a deeper stillness of beauty. She took her place in the family and among neighbours, she was gentle and loving as before, but she spoke very little, and none, not even her mother, asked her any more questions. Perhaps her mother and some of the old and wise people guessed.

Where Kilmeny had been, what she had seen, was beyond ordinary telling. It was a land beyond this world, yet it was not Elfland; a place of peace and light, stillness and joy, where no rain fell or harsh winds blew.

Yet sometimes she spoke a little of that land, or perhaps sang of it like one singing unearthly music. Only those of quick hearing, who heard with the inward ear, could understand; some of the old and wise did understand, and something was held and passed on and long remembered like a tune. "For the airs of heaven played round her tongue" as she spoke of that land "where sin had never been,

"A land of love and a land of light,
Withouten sun or moon or night,
A land of vision it would seem,
A still, an everlasting dream."

She had fallen asleep in a far, green place and awakened to find herself guarded by good beings: not elves or fairies, but perhaps angels. A vision of the future had been given her: a sad sight of the lady who was to be Mary, Queen of Scots (for Kilmeny lived long before that unhappy queen's day). Then she had slept again and awakened in the green glen she knew, and so had come home.

Her beauty grew more and more unearthly, her look was so still and steadfast, neither that of a mortal girl nor a fairy creature; something beyond any poet's dream. Her voice was like a melody floating from a far land beyond the sea. The songs she sang were holy, and often she withdrew into some quiet, almost hidden place to sing them.

When she walked in the glen or the wood, by the river or on the hillside, she drew all living creatures around her and brought peace among them. The wildest grew quiet at her voice and came to kneel before her, to be touched by her hand. They played around her with other and timid little creatures, as once in Eden when all creation was new and sinless. There was neither fear nor rage among them. Blackbird and eagle flew together, lamb and wolf roamed side by side. The cattle looked up in wonder longing to know more about this mystery.

For all of them it was like Paradise, for Kilmeny had been to that lost land and had brought back with her some of its peace and joy; that land to which all men long to go and where we may all yet return.

Seven years had passed while Kilmeny was there, seven years before she came back to this world. Now she dwelt with her own people only for a month and a day. There was in her the longing to depart to that far place of peace. And one day she went there, never again to return to this world.

> "Kilmeny on earth was nae mair seen,
>   It wasna her hame and she could not remain."

And so she went to the land of light to dwell there until the end of time.

The Wise Woman of Duntulm

There was a poor widow once who lived at Duntulm in the isle of Skye. She had not always been poor, for it was good land on her croft and when her husband and their two fine sons were living all went well. But sorrow fell upon her: one day, suddenly, her husband was drowned in a storm; not long after, her two sons were out in their boat, a squall came up and the boat sank. They were neither of them found.

Mairi, the poor widow, was as brave as a woman could be and did all she could, but she had not strength enough to work the croft. She had to sell all her cows but one, in order to pay the rent and other dues, and just when she thought everything was paid the laird's factor or agent came demanding more. He said that other taxes were due, but did not bother to explain what they were; probably he could not, and was merely trying to get more money out of her.

"I have nothing to give," the poor woman told him, and the factor could believe that when he looked round her poor, bare bit of a place.

"Have you no cattle?" he demanded.

"Only the one cow," she replied.

"Well, I'll take the cow," he said, "and that will pay your dues."

Off went the factor with the cow on a rope, himself riding a pony. After shutting them into a field he went to a friend's house for dinner and a dram. Meanwhile, some decent young men, friends of Mairi's sons, had gone to see her and heard her story. They were full of pity for her, of anger against the factor, and of glee at the thought of a ploy, for they had the idea of getting back the cow.

They went into the field, which had a high wall and was not over-looked from the house where the factor was eating his dinner; one took the cow, another the pony, and off they went down to the shore where their boat was tied up ready to be pushed out. It was a big boat and they took the cow and the pony over to the islet of Pladda where they left the creatures peacefully grazing. Then the lads rowed back.

"We'd better ask the wise woman what to do next," one said to the others. This was a woman they knew well for her wisdom and her kindness. She knew more than most.

"Will you help us to fool the factor?" they asked her.

"Indeed and I will," she assured them. "Off you go now, and meet him and bring him here. But first—let me have one of your bonnets."

Off the lads went, laughing to themselves but keeping a solemn face. They met the factor by the field. He had had a good dinner and a good dram with it, and a bit of a sleep after it; and now he was staring into the empty field where he had left the cow and the pony. The young men gave him a respectful "Good day".

"I don't know what to make of this," said the factor. "I left my pony and a cow I am taking to be sold, safely here in the field—and where are they now?"

"You'd better be asking the wise woman," one of the young men told him. "She may be able to help you—if you speak her fair."

"Would you like us to take you to her?" asked another lad, and the factor agreed.

When they saw the wise woman they could hardly keep from gasping and laughing. She was a very comely woman, her grey hair neatly dressed. She usually wore a white apron and a white mutch or cap. But now she had let down her long hair, one lock hanging over her face. On her head was the bonnet, a big rough one, lent her by one of the lads. Instead of her clean white apron she wore a goatskin she must have had in the house, with a straw rope for a belt. She was glaring at them from under the bonnet and she looked like a witch.

The lads enjoyed this; the factor did not.

"Good wife, can you tell me where are the cow and the pony I left in the field?" he asked.

Without replying, the wise woman came close to him.

"To whom do they belong, the cow and the pony?" she demanded.

"The pony to myself, the cow to the king," replied the factor.

"To the king? That I do not believe at all. How can a cow on this island belong to the king who is so far from here?"

"It belonged to the widow who gave it to me, to sell, and pay her taxes with the money."

"That is not true either. She did not give it to you, you took it from her, and there was no more money due from her. Now I know the meaning of the strange things I saw today."

The wise woman looked very solemn and stern; her voice grew deep and harsh. The young men kept their eyes on the ground, they too looking solemn.

"First of all," went on the wise woman, "I heard a noise in the air, louder than any flight of birds, than any storm of wind. When I looked out, I saw a great fire, as if all the fires on the island were blazing together in one; and going through the fire were the cow and the pony with a host of little men, thousands of them: the Men of the Hill, the Little People whom it is better not to watch. They were driving the cow and the pony to their own place, within that hill yonder. Now, if you like, you may go and find the beasts. And if you can bring them back, you will maybe not take again that which does not belong to you."

The factor drew back from her in terror. Far from going towards the hill, he turned and ran as fast as his legs could carry him back to his own house.

When he had gone the lads had their laugh, and they thanked and praised the wise woman who looked at them very kindly.

"Off with you now," she told them, and off they went, down to the shore, out in their boat, over to Pladda where the cow and the pony were peacefully grazing. They brought the creatures back, no one seeing them, and went up to Mairi's house. She gave them the thanks of her heart and a great blessing. The wise woman was with her and they were having a bite and a sup together.

"Sit you down now, and welcome," Mairi told the good lads, and they all had their bite and sup together.

The cow was lowing peacefully in her shed. The pony was turned loose and no doubt went back to its stable. No one asked about that.

From that day the factor went in fear of the wise woman and of them who, she had said, had taken away the cow and the pony. If he did not become a kind and honest man, at least he became careful and did not take that which did not belong to him.

Colonel MacNeill's Brownie

A Brownie or house-fairy is a useful friend, kind to good housewives, helping them by night in kitchen and dairy. This particular Brownie, a female one, did more than that. She was the protector of Colonel MacNeill of Cariskey and his family, and used to follow him into battle. Once, when a bullet went through the crown of his hat (an inch or so lower, and it would have gone through the crown of his head and made an end of him) he jumped high from the ground, turned round and saw her.

"It is well for me that you were here," he said.

"Indeed and it is," agreed the Brownie.

When he was home again, MacNeill used to ride into Campbeltown and back, and the Brownie liked to ride with him. Usually he enjoyed her company, but one day, whether she was chattering too much, or he was tired or out of temper, or whatever, he threw her off his horse; but he was not rid of her. She went ahead of him, the likes of her not needing a horse, and waited in a wood. As he came past, she gave him a good, hard slap in the face. He was civil to her after that.

She took as good care of his house as of himself, keeping an eye on the maids, to make sure they did their work properly. When guests were expected she was very exacting indeed, for she had the good name of the house at heart and would not have MacNeill put to shame by any negligence.

A careless housemaid once went to bed leaving her work half-done; the hearth choked with ashes, dust everywhere, the mirrors and glass doors of book-case and china-cabinet all dim. The girl was half-asleep when she felt a tweak at her curl-papers. It hurt, and she put up her hand. The hand was pinched and smacked. Then the blankets were pulled off her, and she was pushed and poked until, crossly and drowsily, she got out of bed. Another push sent her to the door of her attic and downstairs to the hall where grey ashes lay on the hearth, and a film of dust on the table.

Grumbling, but under her breath for she knew who was behind her, she dared not say a word aloud, the girl cleared and swept the hearth, laid the fire properly, turned round and saw tiny footprints all over the table. The Brownie had deliberately walked across it to show how dusty it was, and she had drawn her fingers across the surface of a mirror and of the glass doors. Yawning and sighing, the maid fetched her duster and polishing cloths, and set to work. Then she stumbled back to bed, but in five minutes, or so it seemed to her, it was time to rise and begin the day's work. She came down, however, to a clean hearth, the fire burning brightly, and to remarkably bright furniture.

The dairymaid, with her pails full of milk, stood by the back door gossiping and flirting with a farm lad who should have been at work in the field, while the girl should have taken the milk to the dairy. The lad snatched a kiss, the lass squealed; she squealed again but not with pleasure when a small hard hand smacked her on the cheek. Two hands took her by the shoulders, turned her round and pushed her off to the dairy; there she must stay until the churning was done. The butter came quickly, and it was good, firm, sweet butter; there was a thick layer of cream too, on the pans set aside for creaming.

The scullery-maid was cuffed if the dishes, pots and pans were not perfectly clean, the cloths all washed, wrung and hung out to dry. The laundry-maid felt the sting of the Brownie's hand if she made the faintest scorch on the linen or left a tiny crease. Even those important personages, the cook and the housekeeper, did not escape; they were not smacked but they were chivvied, made to feel a cold draught, pushed about. And they were admonished when necessary.

"The oven's too hot," a sharp voice would tell the cook. "Don't forget the salt—the nutmeg—some herbs—more sugar."

The cook soon realized that the criticism was sound.

As for the housekeeper, she liked to settle down with a cup of tea, her feet on a stool, her eyes closed in thought (or could it be in sleep?) for half an hour or so; but there would be a sharp reminder that she had not gone through her stores in the cupboard, or her sheets and towels in the linen-room. It became acutely uncomfortable to sit there drinking her tea, or trying a new pattern in knitting, or just sitting. She was compelled to bustle off to her store-room, to make sure that none of jam or the bottled fruit had gone sour or sugary, that there was an ample supply of all provisions and preserves, to find what linen needed mending, to see that there were pillow-cases and towels, big and little, enough, for all the bedrooms, that the napkins matched the table-cloth. Although she might grumble in thought, and sigh a bit, she had to admit the result was worth it.

"There's never a house so warm and comfortable as yours," one guest would say. Another sighed with pleasure at finding a bright fire in her room, hot water in a big, shining can, soft, warm towels, and at bedtime, a warm bed with satin-smooth sheets and pillows, all fragrant with lavender.

"This is the best broth—the lightest pastry—the finest dinner altogether," people would say, coming back for second helpings, and there was always enough for that.

"I wish your dairy-maid would teach mine to make butter. Would your cook give me her recipe for this cake?"—and so on.

MacNeill looked modest, but he could almost be heard purring.

The guests were lavish with praise, and lavish with tips, being kindly and grateful folk. The Brownie rightly took much of the praise to herself. The tips did not interest her; Brownies care nothing for money. These all went to the servants, who were gratified.

Colonel MacNeill beamed with pleasure: "It's all thanks to you," he said in a low voice. The Brownie heard, and gave a little laugh. So all of them were happy.

20

The Red Etin

There were once two poor widows who lived near each other. One had two sons, the other only one. The three lads were decent and brave and very good friends. Which of them was the best and wisest this story will show.

There was little to do in the place where they lived and they often spoke of going out into the world to seek their fortune. One day the elder of the two brothers told his mother he must go.

"Then take this pitcher to the well and draw water, and I'll bake you a bannock for food on your way."

The lad went to the well; his mind was so set on his adventure that he did not notice that the jug was cracked, letting some of the water out. He brought back only enough to mix a wee bannock.

"Will ye have half o't wi' my blessing, or the whole o't without my blessing?" asked his mother.

"It's little enough as it is," said the lad. "I'll not travel far on that. I'll have the whole bannock." He put the bannock into his pocket and off he went, without his mother's blessing. Before he left, he gave his brother a knife.

"Take a look at it every day. As long as I'm safe and well, the knife will be bright; but if I'm in danger or distress, it will be dull and rusty."

The lad walked all that day and the next. On the third day he came to a field where a shepherd was pasturing his flock.

"Whose sheep are these?" the lad asked him, and the shepherd answered, half speaking, half singing the words:

> "The Red Etin of Ireland
>   Aince lived in Ballygan,
>   And stole King Malcolm's daughter,
>   The King of fair Scotland.
>
> "He beats her, he binds her,
>   He lays on her a band,
>   And every day he dings her
>   With a bright silver wand.
>   Like Julian the Roman,
>   He's ane that fears no man.
>
> "It's said there's ane predestinate
>   To be his mortal foe;
>   But that man is yet unborn,
>   And lang may it be so."

This was not very helpful. The lad went on and after a while came to a field where another older man was herding pigs. He asked whose they were and was told it was the Red Etin. Farther on, he came to a field where a still older man had a herd of goats. From him the lad had the same answer, but with some advice as well:

"Beware of the next beasts ye meet. They'll be fearsome."

That, indeed, they were: cattle with two heads, and on each head four horns. They roared and came at him, and he fled, as fast as he could. Coming to a castle with an open door, he dashed inside. An old woman was there, sitting by the fire. She looked poor and sad and wretched, but not unkind, and the lad begged her to hide him and give him shelter for the night.

"Bide if ye will, but ye'd be safer outbye, better as far frae here as you can travel, for this is the castle of the Red Etin and he is mair fearsome than any beast ye'll meet."

"I'll chance that. Only hide me."

The old woman shut him into a cupboard, only a minute before a great roaring and stamping were heard, and a dreadful voice called out (or rather, three voices all roaring together):

> "Snouk but and snouk ben,
>   I find the smell o' an earthly man;
> Be he living or be he dead,
>   His heart this nicht shall kitchen my bread."

The cupboard door was opened and the poor lad dragged out. He saw a fearsome giant with three heads, and three mouths roaring at him.

"I'll spare ye, if ye can answer three questions," said one of the heads, and then it asked:

"What is the thing that has neither beginning nor end?"

The second head asked:

"What is the thing which, the smaller it is, is the more dangerous?"

The third head asked:

"When do we see a dead thing carry the living?"

None of these questions could the poor lad answer. The Red Etin hit him on the head with his club, and he was turned to stone and bundled away.

Meanwhile, at home, his brother had looked every day at the knife. One morning it was dull and rusty.

"Some ill has befallen my brother," he told their mother. "I must away and find him."

"First bring me water from the well and I'll bake ye a bannock for the journey," she said.

The lad took the old pitcher, not noticing the crack, went to the well and brought the jug back half empty. There was only enough water to mix a wee bannock.

"Will ye have this without my blessing, or half o't wi' my blessing?" asked his mother.

"I'll have it all. It's little enough," he said, and off he went, like his brother, without his mother's blessing.

Following the same way he came to the pasture where the shepherd kept his flock, asked him who owned the sheep and was given the answer that the shepherd had given his brother. So too it happened with the swineherd and the goatherd who added his warning about the fearsome beasts. The lad met those two-headed eight-horned cattle and fled in terror, rushed into the castle and begged the old woman to hide him. This she did though she warned him as she had his brother. The Red Etin came roaring and stamping in, uttering his rhyme; he dragged the poor lad out from his hiding-place, put the same three questions, and when the lad could not answer, struck him to stone and bundled him away like one dead.

At home, their comrade, the only son, wondered what had happened to them, and one day told his mother:

"Mother, I must away after my comrades, for I fear some ill has befallen them."

"First bring me water from the well and I'll bake ye a bannock for the journey," she said.

The pitcher the lad took to the well was cracked like the other one, but a raven on the tree above the well croaked out to him: "Look at the crack."

"Thank you kindly," said the lad. He patched it with some moist clay, filled it full and brought it back. There was enough water to bake a fine big bannock.

"Will ye have it all or will ye have half o't wi' my blessing?"

"I wouldna go without your blessing," he said, and his mother blessed him and gave him the half bannock.

Off he went and walked a long way, then sat down to eat his bannock.

"Will ye spare me a bit of your bannock?" asked a feeble voice, and there stood a little old woman, bent and grey and wrinkled.

"I will, and gladly," the kind lad told her, and he broke the bannock in two.

The old woman ate her share, and it was like magic food. There she stood, no longer a poor little old wifie, but young and lovely, a fairy woman and a good fairy.

"For your kindness I will help you," she said in a sweet voice. "Take this wand, and listen to me, while I tell you what you must say and do."

The lad took the wand and listened gratefully. Then the fairy vanished and he went on his way, with a high heart.

Presently he came to the pasture and asked whose sheep these were.

The shepherd answered, as before, half singing the words:

"The Red Etin of Ireland
  Aince lived in Ballygan,
  He stole King Malcolm's daughter,
  The King of fair Scotland.

He beats her, he binds her,
  He lays on her a band,
  And every day he dings her
  With a bright silver wand.
  Like Julian the Roman,
  He's ane that fears no man."

Then he sang a different verse from the one he had sung to the other two lads:

"But now I fear his end is near,
  And destiny at hand;
  For you're to be, I plainly see,
  The heir of all his land."

This was good to hear, and the lad went cheerfully on. The swineherd and the goatherd gave him the same answer, and the goat herd warned him about the fearsome beasts. These great two-headed, eight-horned cattle came at him but he stood firm; he struck one of them with his wand, and it fell dead. The others fled away.

The lad went into the castle and spoke courteously to the old woman. The Red Etin came roaring and rushing in, but the lad again stood firm.

The first head asked the question:

"What is the thing that has neither beginning nor end?"

"A bowl," answered the lad.

The second head asked:

"What is the thing which, the smaller it is, is the more dangerous?"

"A bridge," said the lad.

The third head asked: "When do we see a dead thing carry the living?"

"When we see a ship sailing, with men on board," the lad told him, answering these three questions as the fairy woman had bidden him.

The Red Etin knew that a magic stronger than his own had overcome him. He collapsed on the floor. The lad drew his sword and cut off the three horrible heads, one after the other. Then he dragged heads and body to the edge of the cliff on which the castle stood, and pushed them over into the sea which swirled and billowed at the foot. And that was the end of the Red Etin.

The old woman looked very kindly at him when he came back to the castle.

"Come you with me," she said and led him up a great staircase and along a gallery with doors on either side. These opened one by one and from each came a beautiful girl. From the last door came the loveliest of them all, the daughter of the king. All of them had been stolen and held captive by the Red Etin and now his death had broken the spell. At the end of the gallery stood two figures, stiff as figures of stone. These were the two brothers, luckless, foolish lads who had so heedlessly set forth on their adventures without their mother's blessing.

Their comrade, remembering what the fairy woman had told him, struck them with his wand, and they came to life.

They all gathered round their rescuer, thanking him, rejoicing in their freedom and in the destruction of the Red Etin. The old woman, herself taken captive more years ago than she could remember, made a good supper for them and the three lads found the cellar full of rare wine. They slept in the castle and next morning rode away, for the

Red Etin had a stable full of horses. They took the old woman and all the girls with them.

Before very long they reached the palace of the king who was overcome with joy and thankfulness at finding his daughter, whom he thought he had lost for ever, safe and well. The other ladies were daughters of noblemen in the city and kingdom and very soon the news was proclaimed and their parents came to rejoice.

"I vowed that the man who rescued my daughter should have her as his bride," proclaimed the king. This pleased both the princess and the lad. His comrades too found each a bride among the girls who had been released from enchantment.

Already the three lads had sent a messenger to tell their mothers the end of the adventure and to give them the invitation from the king to come to his court. This they gladly did. They were welcomed with great kindness and courtesy and made chief guests at the wedding-feast. To each of them and to the old woman from the castle the king gave a fine house with servants to look after them.

So everyone was happy. The feasting went on for many days, the happiness for more years than can be counted. Indeed it may well be that they are living yet, and still very happy.

21

The Sea Maiden

A poor old fisherman sat in his boat, fishing but catching nothing; his luck had been bad that year and for many a day. So, when a sea maiden rose out of the waves by his boat and asked him was he catching many fish, he answered sadly:

"No indeed, it is very little I have caught today or yesterday or for many a day."

"What will you give me if I send you a good catch?"

"Och, it's little I have to give."

"Will you give me your first son?"

"My son? I have none, and am not likely to, for my wife and I are old."

"What have you then?"

"Only an old mare and an old dog are with me, and my old wife."

"Here then," said the sea maiden, "take these grains. Three you will give to your wife, three to your mare, three to your dog; and three you will plant behind your house tonight. In time, your wife will have three sons, your mare three foals, your dog three puppies, and from the seeds you plant will grow three trees. The trees will be to you a sign of your sons' welfare. If one of them should die, his tree would wither. Off with you and do what I have told you; I will see to it that you have good fishing, and you, when your eldest son is three years old, must remember me."

The fisherman promised, and then he went home and did as the sea maiden had bidden him. From that day he prospered, having many a great catch of fish. In a year's time a son was born to him and his wife; in two years, another son, in three years a third. The mare had her three foals, the dog her three puppies, and three trees were growing behind the house.

But the old fisherman was not happy, for he remembered the sea maiden's demand for his eldest son. On the fourth anniversary of the day he had met her, there she was again.

"Have you brought me your son?" she asked.

"Och, but I'm the careless and foolish one! I forgot this was the day," said the old man.

"Did you now? Well, you may keep him for four years more, and the good fishing will go on," said the sea maiden.

The fisherman thanked her humbly and went home. All went well for four years. The boys grew and were strong, the three foals and the three puppies grew, the three trees flourished. The old man and his wife were well content—until the day drew near for him to take his son to the sea maiden. The day came, the maiden rose out of the sea and asked:

"Have you brought me your son?"

"Och, and I am the foolish and forgetful one, and it is sorry I am but I forgot."

"Well, I'll let you have him for seven years more; but then indeed I must have him."

To the old man seven years appeared a long time; he would surely be dead before they were over, and need not trouble any more. All went well with him and his family, but as the seventh year was near its end he began to be sad and troubled. His eldest son asked what ailed him—for they were all well in health, and the fishing was good. The father would not say, but the lad kept on asking, and at last his father answered him. The day was very near.

"Then I'll go with you," declared the son.

"You will not," said his father. "I will not give you up."

They argued for a time, then the son said:

"Well, if you will not let me go with you to the sea maiden, take me to the smith, and bid him make me a sword. Then I'll go off into the wide world to seek my fortune."

The father agreed to that and went to the smith, who forged a good sword. But when the lad drew it and gave it a swing or two, it broke into fragments.

"Och, that will not do at all," he said.

The smith made another, a strong, well-tempered sword, but when the lad drew it and tried it, it too broke. A third time the smith set to work, and this time he forged a sword so strong and heavy that few men could have wielded it; but the lad did, and it pleased him, for it did not break.

So he set out into the world to seek his fortune, riding one of the three foals which was now his own good horse, and followed by one of the puppies which was his own dog.

When he had ridden for a time he came upon a dead sheep; beside it were gathered a fox, an otter and a falcon. The lad alighted from his horse, and with his sword swiftly divided the carcass, giving three parts to the fox, two to the otter and one to the falcon, which seemed to them fair sharing and saved trouble. They thanked the lad.

"For your kindness to me I will do you service," promised the fox. "If ever you are in need of swiftness of foot or sharpness of tooth call me and I will come."

"And if you need one that can swim, call me and I will come," promised the otter.

"If swift wings and strong claws can ever save you, call me and I will come," said the falcon.

The lad thanked them and rode on, his dog following. They came to a king's palace and there he took service as a herd-boy. He was to have food and wages according to the milk the cattle gave. The first day he found but bare pasture, and they gave very little milk, so his food and payment were poor. Next morning he led them farther, and came to a fine green glen where the pasture was the best he had ever seen. The cattle grazed their fill, and in the evening the lad was about to drive them home, sure of his wages and his supper, when a great and hideous giant came down upon him with a roar of rage.

"This is my pasture and the cattle that have fed on it are mine; and you are mine, and I will have your head off you."

"Oh, will you?" said the lad. "There may be two ways about that."

He drew his word and they fell to fighting. His good dog came with him, and at the height of the fighting leaped upon the giant's back, making him bend his head. The lad swept his sword and cut the giant's head clean off.

He went home then, but first he found the giant's castle and it was full of gold and jewels; but the lad took nothing. He went back to the king's palace, and the cattle were milked, giving such a yield that the king was well pleased, and the lad had a fine supper and much praise. Next day, and for some days to come, he took his cattle to the green glen of good pasture, and all was well. But in time the cattle had grazed the ground bare and he led them farther, to another glen of good pasture, and here the same adventure befell him; at evening, as he was leading the cows home, a great giant came roaring at him, but the lad answered and defied him, and went at him with his sword. This giant too he killed, striking off his head. Back to the king his master's house he led the cows, and the milking that night was indeed rich. For a time, all went well. The king and queen thought they had never had such a herd-boy and everyone liked the lad, who was well content.

But one evening he came home, the cattle well fed, likely to give plenty of milk, and found no welcome but a sadness upon everyone. The dairymaid told him with tears that a frightful, three-headed monster had come up out of the loch. It came every year, demanding a victim; and this year it was to be the princess, the king's own, only daughter.

"That isn't right at all," said the lad.

"Indeed it is not," agreed the dairymaid. "But there is a powerful, brave knight that thinks the same as you, and he is coming to rescue the princess, and if he does, he is to marry her."

"Is he now?" said the lad.

Next day the champion arrived, talking loudly of what he would do. He led the princess out to the loch, and waited. Out of the waters, with a churning and a hissing and steaming, came a horrible monster— not a sea-serpent, not a beast of prey, but a bit of both, with three heads, each uglier than the other. The poor princess came near to fainting, and the brave champion ran away. The monster approached, but just at that moment another champion came riding, his dog following him. He was a handsome youth in goodly armour, with a great sword; it was the herd-boy himself, wearing a suit of armour he had found in the giant's castle.

"Let you not be afraid of that great ugly monster, my princess," he said in a gentle, courteous voice. "I will help you if I can. Will you stand back there, by that tree?"

Then he rushed at the monster and swirled his sword. It was a sore fight, but he won. His good horse helped him and so did his dog, and he cut off one of the three hideous heads. This was not the end of the monster, for there were two other heads which set up a frightful yelling and howling, as the creature shambled back into the loch. The princess was crying with gratitude.

"Och now, don't be crying like that," said the lad cheerfully, as he tied up the head with a withy, or willow stem. "Will you carry this at your saddle, back to the king your father, to reassure him? I must leave you."

The princess smiled on him and gave him a ring from her finger. He helped her into her saddle, hung the head by her and rode off—to lay aside his armour, get into his rough clothes and go back to the herding, and bring home his cows for the milking.

As the princess rode home she met the braggart champion, who came up to her in a vile temper, telling her that he would kill her there and then, if she did not give him the monster's head. She did this meekly enough, but did not tell him what was in her mind. He would not have liked it. There was rejoicing in the palace, and the king and everyone else gave the false knight great praise for his rescue of the princess.

But the monster still had two heads and they would each demand a victim and vengeance. This had not happened before, because a poor maiden had always been sacrificed. So next morning the false knight must ride out again with the princess.

He was terrified, but the princess was torn between fear and hope. Might not that unknown brave rescuer come again?

The two-headed monster appeared, looking even more fearsome for the loss of one head, and the cowardly knight fled. He had hardly disappeared before the brave lad came to comfort the princess. It was a sore fight; the monster was in a frightful rage and had lost none of his power. But at last he was overcome, and the lad cut off another head; he was nearly exhausted, and had just strength enough to tie up the head with a withy, hang it on the princess's saddle and himself ride away. She thanked him with all her heart and gave him an earring. It is doubtful if he could have won without the help of his good dog and his horse who carried him very carefully.

Again the princess was met by the false champion, again threatened if she told the truth, and again he seized the monster's head as proof of his claim to have fought and won.

There was praise for him, there was more rejoicing, but the king knew that there must be a third conflict which might finally destroy the monster. And this time the fearsome creature came up with a hissing and a roar of pain terrifying to hear; he was more than ever fearsome to look at with two great bloody patches where once had been two heads. The false knight yelled with fear and fled.

The princess waited bravely—only for a moment—for there came her true champion riding his horse, followed by his dog. Never had she seen anyone so steadfast. The dreadful fight was resumed, and it was worse and longer than before, with moments when the princess could not bear to look. The lad fought bravely, his good dog and his horse helped, but the monster frantic with pain and rage seemed to have gained strength. But he could not hold out, and in the end the brave lad, with one last sweep of the sword he was almost too exhausted to hold, cut off the third head. There it lay on the ground and beside it the dead monster.

Weeping with gratitude, the princess spoke very sweetly to her

rescuer and gave him the other earring. This he put carefully away
with its fellow and with the finger-ring. He helped the princess on to
her horse, bound the head with a withy and hung it on the saddle and
himself rode back to his herding.

For the third time the false knight met the princess, and threatened
her with death if she did not give him the head and keep silence. She
obeyed, keeping her thoughts to herself. This time there was rejoicing
without any more fear. The three heads were there to prove that the
monster was finally slain.

The king, whatever he felt about it, had to keep his word, so he
announced the wedding for the next day.

The princess did not weep or rebel. She only said:

"I will marry the man who can untie the heads from the withies."

That, the king thought, was as good as agreeing to marry the knight,
and the knight thought so too; but he could not undo even one of the
heads from its withy. After that every man about the place tried his
hand, but none of them could do it. Last of all came the herd-laddie,
just back with his cows; and in a flash and a flash and a flash he had
untied all the three heads. The king was not best pleased—but he was
a man of his word. He was well pleased, though, next day, when he
found that the false champion had taken himself off, and the true hero
came to his wedding richly dressed, and bringing fine gifts to the king,
and jewels for his bride, all taken from the giant's treasury.

So they were married and lived happily together; but that is not the
end of the story. There was danger still for both of them, and strong
magic about them. Perhaps the sea maiden had a hand in it—who
knows? Anyhow, one day as they were walking by the loch, another
fearsome beast came out of it and carried off the bridegroom. The
princess wept; then she went to consult the blacksmith who was a
wise man. He told her to bring her finest jewels to the lochside and lay

them out. This she did, and the monster came out of the water, with a covetous look.

"These are fine jewels you have," it said.

"I will give them to you if you will bring back my husband."

The monster agreed, brought back her husband, and went off with the jewels. They were happy together for a little while longer; then one day as they walked by the loch, the monster arose again and seized the princess. Her husband was in bitter grief; he too went to the wise old smith, who told him that his wife was held captive on an island in the middle of the loch. On the island, too, was a white hind of incredible swiftness; and in the hind was a hoodie crow that could fly very swiftly, and in the crow a trout, and in the trout an egg.

"And in the egg is the soul of the monster," said the smith. "If you can take and break it, you will destroy the monster and save your wife. But it will be a sore fight, and you will need help, I'm thinking."

The brave lad rode his good horse down to the shore and the horse took one clean leap on to the island, the brave dog following. There they saw the hind, which fled so swiftly that the horse could not come up with her.

"If I had but that fox I met the day I set out," said the lad, "he would be swift enough to catch the hind."

And there the fox was, rushing after the hind and catching her! Out of her flew a hoodie crow, flying away swiftly.

"And here I want the falcon," said the lad; and the falcon came swooping with the hoodie crow in her beak! Then out of the crow came a trout which plunged deep into the loch.

"Och, now I need the otter," cried the lad; and the otter was there, flashing into the water, coming up with the trout in her mouth. The egg dropped out of the trout, and the lad put his foot upon it.

The monster was there, howling for mercy.

"Give me back my wife," demanded the lad.

"I will—here she is."

And there stood the princess.

But the lad, knowing the evil of the monster and the great power of danger and magic about them, caught her in his arms, while he pressed his foot hard on the egg; it broke, the monster fell dead, and that was the end of him or her, whichever it was.

But it is not yet the end of the story. This hero had still an adventure to come. One day he and the princess were walking in the wood, and he saw a dark castle.

"Who bides there?" he asked.

"I do not know; but it is someone of great power and magic and evil. So do not think of going to it," begged the princess.

"If there is evil, it must be destroyed," said the prince, as he now was, for he was heir to the king her father. And he went off to the castle. He was met by a little old woman who was, you may guess, a most evil and powerful witch. She spoke him fair, bidding him enter before her, to be welcomed with honour. As he passed she struck him with a magic wand, and laid him as if dead on the ground. There was much woe in the palace that night. There was woe also in the fisherman's house, for one of the three trees had withered, and they knew that meant that ill had befallen the eldest son.

"Now I must go to rescue him," vowed the second brother. He went to the smith, had a good sword forged, and rode off on his own horse with his own dog following. He found the tracks of his brother, no doubt he heard news of him on the way, and at last he came to the palace and presented himself. There he learned of the last evil spell and went off to the castle. But it happened to him as to his brother; he was met and beguiled by the old woman, and struck with her magic wand. So his tree too was seen to wither. The third brother said:

"Now I must go and rescue both my brothers."

He in turn rode off on his horse armed with a good sword, and followed by his dog. When he came to the castle he met the witch who bade him enter. But this lad was more cautious than his brothers. He drew back.

"It is you who must go first," he said.

Stepping behind her he cut off her head with his sword; but the witch picked it up and put it on again as if it had been a bonnet, and turned to attack him. His dog came to help him but the witch struck the dog with her wand and laid him stiff as a stone upon the ground. After a fierce fight, the lad managed to get hold of the wand, and struck the witch. She fell, stiff as a stone, on the ground. The lad entered the castle where he found his two brothers lying stone-like, as if dead.

"Maybe the wand that struck them will bring them back to life," he thought, and touched them both. They rose at once, alive and well. They followed him out of the castle. He touched his good dog and brought him, too, back to life, leaping up and wagging his tail.

"Maybe now that she has lost her wand, she can be killed," he thought. He cut off the witch's head, and this time she did not move at all, but lay headless and dead.

The three lads went back to the palace and of the rejoicing there was no end; the evil magic was overcome. The eldest made a great banquet for his brothers and loaded them with treasures. They too found each a lovely and gentle bride, among the princess's ladies.

After the weddings they all returned to their old mother and father to comfort them, and set them up in a good house, well stored and furnished, with a kind servant or two to look after them.

No more harm befell any of them. They lived happily, indeed they may all be living yet, in their country beyond the waves, full of peace and joy.

22

The Good Housewife

There was a good housewife once whose name was Inary. You could not have found any fault in her work. Her house was clean and warm, there was always a store of food in the cupboard, her linen chest was well filled. Her spinning-wheel was rarely silent, or if it were she was weaving at her loom. Indeed she was, if anything, too busy, taking little rest, up early and sitting late at night to finish some task.

One night, long after her husband was in bed, asleep, she was at her loom trying to finish a piece of cloth she was weaving. Tired to the bone, half asleep, she hardly knew what she was saying when she murmured to herself:

"Och, if only someone would come from near or far, from land or sea, to help me finish this web of cloth."

There was a knock at the door, and a voice cried: "Inary, good housewife, let me in, and I'll help you to finish your work."

That sounded fine, so Inary opened the door. In came a woman dressed in green who, without another word, went to the loom and took up the task of weaving. Hardly had Inary shut the door than there was another knock, and another voice cried:

"Inary, good housewife, let me in and I'll work for you."

Another woman came in and sat down at the spinning-wheel. Then a third came who took up the distaff; and a fourth who began helping her to card the wool. There were enough of them now for all the work Inary wanted and more; but that was not the end. Again and again came a knock at the door, and the cry: "Let me in, good Inary, and I'll work for you." The kitchen was full of them and full of the noise and whirr of wheels. One of them boiled water for fulling the newly woven cloth, others pulled it and rolled it, the spinning and carding went on. How her husband slept on through all the din, Inary could not think.

As for herself she was kept busy. There was no spinning or weaving or any work of that kind for her to do, but the visitors demanded food and she dared not refuse them. So she hung her girdle or gridiron over the fire and began baking piles of good oatmeal bannocks; she brought butter and cheese and milk from her stores and served her guests. They ate all she offered, and demanded more. The poor woman was nearly dead with tiredness, far more weary than before, and she was nearly deafened by the noise of whirring wheels. It could surely be heard for a mile and more, yet her husband slept on, in his bed beyond the partition. Inary went to him, shook him, stripped off the blankets, screamed in his ear—but he did not stir. He slept as if he had drunk a cup of drugged ale or wine, or had been put under a spell.

Inary could bear it no longer. She ran out of the house. Those Other People were, for the moment, too busy to notice her going and they had had enough to eat. Indeed there was hardly any food left.

She went straight to the house of a wise man she knew, and begged his advice.

"Aren't you the foolish woman, Inary," he told her, "inviting the likes of Them into your house? They will not come without being bidden, but once they are in they will not easily be put out. They will help you, but they will make you pay. Have you never been told that? You have asked for what you should not, and how indeed you are paying for it. But look, I can tell you what to do."

"Indeed and I have been foolish," admitted Inary humbly. "I'll never do this again, once I'm rid of Them."

The wise man told her what to do, and she listened carefully. Then she ran back to her house. There she stood on a hillock near the door and cried out, as the wise man had bidden her:

"Burg Hill is on fire. There is fire in Burg Hill."

Now Burg Hill was the dwelling of those Other People. The door of Inary's house opened, and out streamed her visitors crying and wailing:

"The Hill is on fire, and my children are burning."

"My cattle and horses will be burned."

"My meal-chest, my distaff, my spinning-wheel will all be destroyed."

They streamed past Inary taking no notice of her, and she ran into her house, locked and barred the door, and began to do all the things the wise man had bidden her do. She twisted the distaff the wrong way, she took the band of the spinning-wheel so that it could not be turned, she turned the loom upside down, and took the pot off the fire, where the water was boiling for the fulling of the cloth. Then she began baking bannocks with the little meal that was left—and waited. She had not long to wait.

The Other People had gone to Burg Hill and found no fire there. Now they came streaming back, crying out in fury: "Let us in, good Inary, let us in."

"I cannot," replied Inary. "My hands are mixing the meal and water to make bannocks."

Then the People began calling to all the things in the house.

"Let us in, small distaff."

"I cannot," said the distaff. "I am twisted the wrong way."

"Let us in, good spinning-wheel."

"I cannot, for my band is taken off and I cannot turn."

"Let us in, great loom."

"I cannot, for I am turned over and I cannot rise."

Nothing could move. Then the People called to the water in the pot:

"Let us in, let us in."

"I cannot, for the pot is off the fire, and I am off the boil."

By this time the bannocks were baking, and one little bannock was toasting before the fire.

"Good little bannock, kind little bannock, let us in," cried the people.

"I'll do that," said the bannock, and it began trundling to the door. But Inary was too quick for it. She remembered what the wise man had told her about this, she caught up the bannock, broke and ate it. So that was the end of the bannock.

The People outside raged and roared and battered the door. And still Inary's husband slept. Then she recalled the last counsel of the wise man.

"He has been spell-bound by your visitors," he had told her. "To waken him you must pour over him the water that they have boiled for the fulling of the cloth."

Inary took the pot, and emptied it over her husband. He awoke with a yell that was good to hear, rushed to the door and roared at the People who stood outside: roared louder even than they did. They knew then that the spell was broken, their power ended, and they fled. There was silence then, except perhaps for some words spoken by her husband to Inary the good (or foolish) housewife.

Four Historians of the other Country

Robert Kirk

One of the first and greatest of the historians to write about the secret, hidden country and its inhabitants was a scholarly clergyman, the Reverend Robert Kirk who lived three hundred years ago, which is part of real book-history.

He was born in 1640 or 1641 during the Civil War, and lived until 1692, in the reign of William and Mary. The facts are to be found in the records of the Church of Scotland.

He was the seventh child of the Reverend James Kirk, minister of Aberfoyle, Perthshire. A seventh child has often a special gift, an inner sight and knowledge, which this boy undoubtedly possessed. He had a good deal of book-knowledge too, he was a brilliant student at Edinburgh University where he took his degree of Master of Arts, and at St Andrews where he read theology. Aberfoyle is on the borders of the Celtic Highlands, and Robert spoke both Gaelic and

English; he published a Gaelic Psalter and had a share in a Gaelic translation of the Bible.

After being ordained to the ministry Robert Kirk was appointed to the parish of Balquhidder, then succeeded his father in Aberfoyle. There he wrote his unique book, a masterpiece, on *The Secret History of Elves, Fauns and Fairies*. This was left in manuscript, and not published until long after his own day. It is not at all fantastic in style, it is sober, full of detail; it could be an account of some little-known region or race of real human people visited by the writer.

How did he know so much? That question has never been answered. Did he see or hear things that no other mortal knew, did he once look into a fairy hill? That sounds fantastic—but his *Secret History* reads as if he had.

Indeed he knew too much. Those Other People do not care to be watched or questioned, some of them do not even like to have their names known and spoken by humans. They may have been angry with Mr Kirk; they may, on the other hand, have liked him and wanted to have him in their own place. However that may be, he disappeared one day in the year 1692.

Nothing was heard or seen of him afterwards. Some of his congregation either did not believe or did not want to believe or did not want to have it known that he had vanished; so they buried a coffin in the churchyard at Aberfoyle, and set up a tomb with his name and the dates of his life, calling him, in Latin, "The Light of the Gaelic Language".

This stone was seen by Sir Walter Scott (who knew a good deal about elves and fairies himself). In 1815 the manuscript of the *Secret History* was published. Another edition appeared in 1893 with a preface by Andrew Lang who collected and retold so many fairy tales. There has been a new edition recently.

At the time of Mr Kirk's disappearance his wife was expecting a baby. One day Mr Kirk appeared to a friend and gave him a message for a kinsman, Grahame of Duchray.

At the christening of the child who was soon to be born, Grahame must attend. Mr Kirk would appear, and Grahame must throw his knife at him. It is well known that iron is a protection against magic, a breaker of spells. The touch of the knife would set Mr Kirk free and he would stay with his own people.

The baby, a son, was born, the christening took place. The friend had passed on the message to Grahame of Duchray who was present, his knife in his pocket. Mr Kirk did appear, but Grahame—who alone saw him—was too amazed to act. The knife was not thrown—and the minister vanished again, never more to be seen by mortal eyes. His book remains.

These Elves, Fauns and Fairies are, Mr Kirk writes, neither human nor angelic, but of a middle race. Very light and flexible in body, they are of a substance so fine that they can disappear when they will. They feed upon fine liquors and upon the substance or essence of grain; some of them steal the corn from the field to grind into flour and bake into bread. They are skilled in all the domestic arts. Some of them are the Brownies who are very domestic, liking to visit human homes by night and do many useful tasks.

The women are skilled in spinning and weaving and embroidery. The clothes they wear are of most delicate substance, cobwebs, gossamer and rainbow, but they are carefully woven and made. Although they live inside hills, they are no cave-dwellers; "their houses are large and fair".

Their country is a hidden one, "the secret commonwealth", and they guard its secrecy well. While they are not ill-disposed to humans, they are jealous of any spying or interference. When they move house, as they usually do at the beginning of each quarter of the year, they do not care to be seen. It is wise, therefore, for humans to stay within doors at those periods. Some people, who are very infrequent church-goers, come to church at such times in order to gain protection and a blessing from on high. (This is a shrewd clerical comment.)

These Other People, the Good People, the People of Peace as they are often called (for it is as well to speak them fair), marry and have children. Like humans, they are divided into families, and tribes or clans. They like to wear the same fashion of clothes as their mortal neighbours, and in the Highlands may wear the tartan.

Without working malice or mischief, so long as they are left unobserved and in peace, they may bring distress; for they like to have a human nurse for their children, and may steal a young mother away, and keep her for a time. She is always well treated, shown honour—but she is kept from her own children as long as the elfin mother needs her. (There is one story about this in the book: *The Queen of Elfland and Her Nurse.*)

Apart from this habit, and from the Brownies' liking to visit a house and do some work, they are not likely to invade human territory, unbidden. It is, however, dangerous to invite them. This was realized by the Good Housewife, Inary, in another story. (The Brownies come unasked, do their work, and depart.)

So Mr Kirk, that good and learned scholar-minister, knew and told too much about The Secret Commonwealth and its People. They took him and where he is now, none can tell.

James Hogg, The Ettrick Shepherd

Young Robert Kirk may easily have gone down to the Borders when he was a student at Edinburgh University, heard some of the legends there, and learned something about The Secret Commonwealth and the Good People. About eighty years after his departure from this earth, another historian of this Other Country was born: James Hogg, who came to be known, from his home and his calling, as The Ettrick Shepherd. He was a friend and contemporary of Sir Walter Scott: born about 1770 (the precise date is uncertain), living until 1835. His family were very poor, his father a shepherd, and James became a herd-laddie after a very brief period at the parish school. He did learn to read and write and he went on learning; he read anything he could lay hands on and practised writing.

There was time for this, as he watched his flock; and besides he had a rich source of legend and tradition at home from his parents, especially from his mother who knew and could recite more tales and ballads than most of her neighbours, and that was saying a lot—for there were many who still remembered those treasures.

This gift Mrs Hogg inherited from her father, who was known as Will o' Whaup. He had himself met some of the Other People. Coming home once, at dusk, he was met by three tiny boys who begged "up-putting for the nicht". This he willingly promised. "Siccan shreds"— such shreds or scraps as they—would need very little food.

"Whaur dae ye come from?" he asked, and they answered:

"From a place ye dinna ken."

Then they made another request: that he would give them a silver key he had.

"In God's Name whaur cam ye from?" asked Will o' Whaup.

There was no reply. The three tiny boys had vanished. What was this silver key and what lock would it have opened? What is well known is that the Other People do not care to hear the Name of God— and when he spoke that, the little shreds disappeared. His grandson James should have made a poem about that.

As a young man, Hogg was shepherd to Mr Laidlaw of Black House, father of Will Laidlaw, who was Scott's faithful friend and secretary. The Laidlaws introduced him to Scott who was visiting the farm and was collecting material for his *Minstrelsy of The Scottish Borders*. Hogg took Scott to see his mother who told him some of the old tales and songs; but when he published them in his *Minstrelsy* Scott was well scolded by Mrs Hogg. These songs and ballads, she told him severely, were made "for singin' and no' for readin', not to be printed in any book", and besides "they're neither richt spelled nor richt set doun". Scott took his scolding meekly, but I do not think he was at all penitent and it is a good thing for us that he did set those songs and ballads down, and many more besides.

As for Hogg, he began to write tales and poems. He went to Edinburgh and met Scott's son-in-law John Gibson Lockhart and his friend John Wilson or Christopher North (his pen-name). With them he was one of the first contributors to the new *Blackwood's Magazine*.

He published a volume of poems, *The Queen's Wake*, and many other books, including one on *The Diseases of Sheep* was sold steadily and well for a long time.

He was always a real shepherd as well as a poet and man of letters. Most of his later life was spent on his own sheep farm, Altrive in Selkirkshire. There is a nice story about him, that when Scott offered to get him an invitation to the coronation of George IV, Hogg declined. It would mean his missing the sheep fair at St Boswells.

Hogg was one of the literary society of Edinburgh in a brilliant age; he was also, and more continuously, a Borderer, a shepherd, a countryman. But he belonged to another country as well. He knew and visited that Other Country of The Other People and brought back news of it in many a tale and poem. His loveliest poem and his funniest are the sources of two of the tales in this book, *Kilmeny* and *The Witch of Fife*.

Robert Chambers

Another historian, a collector of legends and rhymes, was born near the Borders, in Peebles, that pleasant country town not very far from Edinburgh but also close to the hills; it lies on Tweedside. Robert and his elder brother William were the sons of a weaver who, for a time, was comfortably off. William was born in 1800, Robert in 1802. The brothers were to found the great publishing firm of W. & R. Chambers in Edinburgh. William outlived Robert and wrote his *Life*, including bits of autobiography by Robert. The latter published many books of great interest and value, one on *Traditions of Edinburgh*, a *History of The Rebellion of 1745*, and three volumes of *Domestic Annals of Scotland* in which one may happily browse for hours; and most alluring of all, a collection of *Popular Rhymes of Scotland* which contains much more than rhymes: stories, too, the old tales and legends told by the fireside in Lowland homes, told in good Scots, by old women or wandering story-tellers, by nurses and grannies, to eager listeners. This might be called his History of the Other Country, or Traditions of The Secret Commonwealth.

The Chambers brothers had a happy boyhood in Peebles, their parents were kind and sympathetic, and they were, at first, comfortably off. Peebles was very much a community, very sociable. The well-to-do lived in neat houses, well furnished, and used to give tea-parties, very genteel, about six o'clock, at which songs were sung and the old saying: "Peebles for Pleasure" was proved true. It was true among the poorer people too, in their thatched cottages, one room of which was often given over to the man of the house, a weaver and his loom. Life for them was frugal. Most families kept a cow, and grew potatoes which, with porridge eaten from a wooden bowl, made their chief diet. Fires were of peat, as in the Highlands.

Life was frugal but rich in tradition and folk-lore, which was absorbed by Robert and William. They liked to visit an old aunt because she knew so many tales, so it may really be to her that we owe many of the tales retold in Robert's book.

Peebles was so close to the hills and fields that every morning the townspeople were wakened by the town herd blowing his horn. The cows all followed him down to the river, over the bridge and on to common pasture ground. In the evening they were driven home to their own byres.

The town had its characters, beggars and vagrants some of them. One was Jock Grey who had a store of ballads and songs, and composed one himself, a long one, which brought in the names of local families. Sir Walter Scott knew Jock Grey, and he knew another beggar, Andrew Gemmels, whom he made immortal as Edie Ochiltree in *The Antiquary*. Andrew was an old soldier and had become a king's bedesman or beggar, wearing a blue gown and carrying a bag for the alms of food he was given.

Belief in witches and witchcraft was dying out but some folk took precautions against anyone suspected of uncanny power or knowledge. One way was to cross their fingers when passing the cottage of a supposed witch, or meeting her; another was to throw salt on the fire if such a one came into the house. The postman who had many a long walk, always carried a twig of rowan or mountain ash, for this tree, with its scarlet berries, is well known to be a protection against magic and the Other People.

The boys went to the parish school where Robert was unhappy, under a harsh master, and where the education was narrow. They made up for this at home, reading all the books they could find; and they found many, for their father bought all he could afford and sometimes more. He had a set of *The Encyclopaedia Britannica*.

"It was a new world to me," Robert recollected. "I plunged into it. I roamed through it like a bee."

This father was an amiable character but he would appear to have been rather like Mr Micawber in lack of prudence. His weaving business failed and left the family poor. They left Peebles for Edinburgh, where for a time they had to live very meagrely; then, thanks to Mrs Chambers, a most capable and courageous woman, things began to improve. The boys continued their education, they made their career, they became well-known publishers, solid and prosperous citizens of Edinburgh. But they never forgot their childhood in Peebles, and Robert especially remembered, treasured and collected for posterity the fireside tales and songs and rhymes he had heard as a boy.

John Francis Campbell

The people of the Highlands and the western isles knew a great deal about The Other Country and its inhabitants. They were, most of them, very poor in worldly possessions, lacking in book knowledge, and in knowledge of the actual world beyond their own island or corner of the mainland; but they had a wealth of poetry and legend, of traditional knowledge, a sense of magic and enchantments.

Fortunately for us there was an historian of their enchanted history, who, having heard many of their tales, collected them in a book: in four volumes of *Popular Tales of the West Highlands*. His name was John Francis Campbell, and he was born in 1822, the son of Walter Campbell of Islay. By that time some of the Highland gentry were sending their sons to school in England, and this boy went to Eton (which may seem a long way from the secret country), then to Edinburgh University. When he was grown up he travelled widely, as far as Lapland in the north. He was a great naturalist and geologist, and invented an instrument for recording the intensity of the rays of the sun. J. F. Campbell also held various important government jobs; he was a groom-in-waiting to the Prince Consort, and with all respect to that good man it is difficult to think of his being lured into The Other Country or anywhere near it.

But Campbell himself, the Highland gentleman, scholar and traveller, never forgot his own Highlands and islands, or his boyhood on Islay when marvellous tales had been told him, in Gaelic, by a piper, "the instructor of my boyhood", a kind man remembered with affection and gratitude. He returned to the Highlands as often as he could, and not only to the castles and the great houses of the chiefs and gentry, but to the little, dark, smoky dwellings of the poor crofters and fishermen. Perhaps it was an escape from the grandeur and formality of Buckingham Palace and Windsor, even of Balmoral. Did he ever tell the royal children any of his Highland tales?

He had the Gaelic so it was easy for him to talk to people and win their friendship. He got on well with them. There were inspired story-tellers among them, both men and women. Campbell described one of them, John MacPhee of South Uist, and his house. It had two walls of rough stone, the space between them filled with a layer of peat. The roof was thatched; the thatch, held down by ropes, lay on the inner wall, and one could walk on top of the outer wall. There were two doors, one on each side of the house, both opening into the single room which had its hearth in the centre of the floor, a hole in the roof above to let out the peat-smoke (or some of it). One small window let in a little light to flow through the blue peat-reek.

There were many such houses. In summer, the people did not spend much of their time indoors, but in winter, in the long dark nights, they gathered round the fire to tell their stories of The Other Country.

When Campbell visited John MacPhee he found him, an old man, sitting by the fire, on a stool. A small boy stood beside him, listening entranced, to a story. The boy's mother was boiling and mashing potatoes for her husband's dinner, and the baby was crawling about the floor. Besides this human family there were a cat with her kittens, some ducks and ducklings and a hen, all wandering or fluttering about the place, all warm and contented, hoping for a share of the potatoes and anything else that might be going. Presently three travellers came in, were welcomed, and sat down to wait for the ebbing of the tide in the ford. The story-teller had a good audience.

The light faded, the house was full of smoky shadows, the water of the ford had ebbed slowly, low enough to make crossing possible. Campbell set out with the other three travellers. He waded across the ford, the water coming up almost to his waist, over to Benbecula where he walked on, letting his clothes dry in the wind, his head full of marvels and of tidings of The Other Country.

Notes

Rashiecoat. The story of *Cinderella* is probably one of the first you were told: the lovely girl so harshly treated by her stepmother and stepsisters, befriended by her fairy godmother, and sent to the ball at the palace where the prince falls in love with her, and after that bit of trouble with the slipper, marries her, and they live happily ever after. That version comes from France where the fairy tales are nearly all about kings and queens, princes and princesses and their royal courts: all very grand. In Scotland, both in the Highlands and the Lowlands, we hear about kings and queens, but their kingdoms would appear to be small, their way of life not grand and formal.

In *Rashiecoat*, the Scottish version of Cinderella, there are no jealous stepmother, no ugly stepsisters; their place is taken at the end by the hen-wife's daughter. The hen-wife, a woman who looked after the poultry, comes into more than one tale, sometimes helping, sometimes interfering. Here she was helpful at first, then tried to interfere. Perhaps she, rather than a fairy or a witch, appears in the story because she was one of the household, yet did not live in the house with the other servants. She would have her own cottage beside the poultry yard, so it would be easy for the princess to slip out and consult her without being overheard.

And Rashiecoat does not go to a ball, but to church on Sunday: three Sundays running, with a fine new dress each time. Then comes the incident of the lost slipper, as in *Cinderella*.

Cinderella has been made into a pantomime many times; I wish someone would make a pantomime of *Rashiecoat*.

(Source: Robert Chambers, *Popular Rhymes of Scotland*.)

The Hoodie Crow, The Young King of Easaidh Ruadh, Prince Ian Direach and his Quest, and **The Sea Maiden** come from J. F. Campbell's *Popular Tales of the West Highlands*.

Friendship between the hero and kind birds and beasts is often found; there are evil monsters too, as in *The Sea Maiden*.

One of the loveliest things in *The Young King of Easaidh Ruadh* is the kindness of the three creatures: the dog, the hawk, and the otter. This detail is found in Russian legends too, and so is the secret of where the giant's soul is hidden—like the monster's in *The Sea Maiden*—in an egg. How did the queen know so much? And how did she come to be captive in the Gruagach's house? No one ever bothered to explain; the people who heard this tale and others like it took everything as it came including the ruthlessness.

In more than one story the hero goes over to Erin or Ireland, which always seems much nearer to Scotland and the Western Isles than to England.

The Kingdom of the Green Mountains, The King of Albainn and The Good Lad and **The Wise Woman of Duntulm and the Poor Widow** are from *Waifs and Strays of Celtic Tradition*, edited by Lord Archibald Campbell. **The Two Herdsmen** is also from this source; there are no fairies or Other People here, but a strong belief in ghosts and marvels, which made the servants believe that the hanged man had come down and was pursuing them. *The Wise Woman of Duntulm* comes from the borders, as it were, of the Other Country; no fairies but a belief in them strong enough to be used by the wise woman to frighten the factor.

In *The King of Albainn and the Big Lad* (*A King of Albainn* in Campbell), the Sword of Light screeches as it touches door or window and gives warning of the theft. A spell could be put upon any possessions by an owner who had magic powers. The same thing happens in *Prince Ian Direach*.

Habetrot. This story does not appear to have a moral. In most tales the good heroine is expert and industrious, and so wins a husband. To find one who lacks those virtues is a comfort to any who dislike spinning, sewing, knitting and all such good works. There is another difference too; usually the Other People dislike having their name known and uttered, but Habetrot tells her willingly.

The source of this tale is in a manuscript by Thomas Wilkie—*Old Rites Customs and Ceremonies of the Inhabitants of the Southern Counties* of Scotland: it has been printed in *A Forgotten Heritage: Original Folk Tales of Scotland*, edited by Hannah Aitken. It has also been retold by Joseph Jacobs and by Sir George Douglas.

The Black Bull of Norroway, Whuppity Stourie and **The Red Etin** come from Chambers's *Popular Rhymes of Scotland*. Many stories tell about three brothers who go into the wide world to seek their fortune and always it is the youngest who fares best. *The Black Bull of Norroway* is about three sisters. It is an old tale told to Scottish children for centuries, although it may have been set in Norway. There has always been a close link between these two countries, ever since a Scottish Princess, long ago, married a King of Norway, and perhaps even before that. And the secret country of Norway is not very far and not very different from that of Scotland.

Mr Kirk said in *The Secret History of Elves, Fauns and Fairies* that The Good People or Other People did not like humans to spy upon them or learn their ways. Nor did they care to have their names spoken. That took away some of their power. Sometimes they might help humans, but they always made a bargain and asked a price; as the Goodwife of Kittlerumpit discovered in the story of *Whuppity Stourie*.

The Red Etin has been told for centuries. It was told by the poet Sir David Lindsay to the little Prince who became James V of Scotland.

The three questions differ in different versions but it is always the third lad and he only who can answer them. The clear moral is that a mother's blessing is worth more than a half bannock.

Thomas the Rhymer, The Lady and the Elf Knight, The Queen of Elfland's Nurse, King Orfeo and his Queen and **Tam Lin** all come from old ballads; *Orfeo* from the Shetlands. That of *The Queen of Elfland's Nurse* is only a fragment and has been much expanded here, but within the proper form and pattern of such tales.

Thomas the Rhymer kept the law of silence and so came home again, but only for a time. Tam Lin was happier; his true love broke the spell and made him safe. One of Thomas's rhyming prophecies was about the family of Haig:

> "Tide what may betide, (tide = happen)
> There will be Haigs at Bemersyde."

Thomas the Rhymer was a real person, a Border laird, Thomas Learmont. He lived at Ercildoune which is now called Earlston, by Leader Water. His house, a tower, was not a grand one (even the lairds' houses were not rich and splendid in those days) but it was strong against wind and rain, and against raiding and reiving from over the Border.

Most of the Border chiefs and lairds did a bit of that, now and then, but Thomas Learmont was not much given to that kind of excitement. He was unlike his neighbours, although well liked and respected by them. Indeed there was no more welcome guest for he was a skilled harper, a sweet singer, and a poet with a fine store of ballads and of tales to be told by the fireside. Because he was a maker of poems and rhymes he was known as Thomas the Rhymer. None of the tales he told was stranger than that of his own adventure.

King Orfeo. The magic country of Greece is very old, older even than the Greece of history and of the great epics and drama. From that ancient and inner kingdom comes the story of Orpheus, the most skilled of harpers. His wife, Eurydice, was taken by Pluto, king of the underworld, down to his kingdom of death, a place not of evil or suffering but of shadows. Orpheus followed, his harp slung over his shoulder, came before Pluto and played so compellingly that Pluto let Eurydice return. But he made one condition: she must follow Orpheus, and he must not look back at her.

They set forth like this, both filled with joy. Orpheus remembering the injunction; but when they were very near home, he could not resist looking back to make sure that she was still there. And at once, she vanished, never again to be seen.

The Austrian composer, Gluck, wrote a lovely sad opera about this legend. The story drifted across land and sea, northwards to Shetland, changing in this long voyage. Perhaps it was told by some poet who could not bear to think of those faithful lovers being parted for ever, and who knew the northern legends of mortals being lured into Elfland, but coming home again. So, Orfeo was made a king. Eurydis his queen, and he was allowed to find her and bring her back safely, without conditions. The king of the fairies was more generous than Pluto.

Kilmeny and **The Witch of Fife** are both from poems by James Hogg, in his *Queen's Wake*. No two could be more different and they show how varied his genius was. *Kilmeny* goes beyond any harm or danger because of her utter innocence, the Witch's husband brings all his trouble upon himself. He was a silly old man but his wife, whatever she may have been up to in magic and mischief, was a good wife and would not let him be burned; she probably let him know about it for months if not years to come.